MR LOVE AND JUSTICE

Mr Love and Justice

COLIN MACINNES

ALLISON & BUSBY

Published 1980 by
Allison and Busby Limited
6a Noel Street, London W1V 3RB

For Robert Hayne

British Library Cataloguing in Publication Data

MacInnes, Colin
    Mr Love and Justice.
    I. Title
    823'.9'1F   PR6063.A239M/

    ISBN 0-85031-333-3
    ISBN 0-85031-334-1 Pbk

Printed in Great Britain by
A. Wheaton & Company Limited,
Exeter

MR LOVE

Frankie love came from the sea, and was greatly ill at ease elsewhere. When on land he was harassed and didn't fit in at all. The orders he accepted without question, though a hundred grumbles, from almost any seaman, were hateful to him in a landsman's mouth. There was a deep injustice, somewhere, in all this. Landsmen, in England, depend entirely on the sea: yet seamen, who sustain them, don't regulate the landsmen's lives and have to submit, when landlocked themselves a moment, to all the landsman's meaningless caprices.

At the Dock Board the chief had said there was no ship for Frankie. Those were his words, but his eyes said, 'I get ten pounds from you before I put you in the pool.' But Frankie had only three-pounds-seven from the Labour. At the Labour exchange they'd asked what he could *do*. How to begin to explain to the quite nice young feller in the striped Italian jacket? On a ship he could do anything: off it, nothing, didn't want to—he was all at sea. 'But you can do a bit of labouring, can't you?' said the clerk, quite friendlily. How to tell him that a merchant seaman can be nothing else—that to do nothing else is a first condition of *being* a merchant seaman? The feller, trying to be helpful, had called over Mister someone who'd looked over the papers, said not a word to Frankie but, just in front of him (two feet from his face behind the grille), 'He's young enough for manual labour—twenty-six.' And, 'A bad discharge-book, too: adrift in Yokohama and repatriated at official expense.'

Frankie stepped back and stood there, feeling powerless and sick; and watched the next-comer, an Asian seaman with a turban. The Asian, at the wicket, smiled and smiled, and, as they questioned him, understood less and less. 'Can't you speak proper English?' somebody shouted at him. Frankie, in his days of glory, would hardly have spoken to the Asian at all: but now both of them were sea princes exiled in distress. He stepped up again and said, 'This man speaks *two* languages—ours and his. It's more than you can— think of that!' They answered nothing, said, 'Next, please,' and the Asian still stood and smiled.

Frankie walked out into Stepney, withered and disgusted. The clients round the Labour, apart from being landsmen, were mostly layabouts: professional scroungers such as you couldn't be on board a ship—your mates wouldn't wear it, let alone the officers. He found the Asian standing near, and turned to share with him his deep contempt for London. In the old days, Frankie thought, he and I would have signed on as pirates down by Wapping: and why not? Frankie became aware the Asian was inviting him to share a meal. 'I'm skint,' said Frankie, not because he was but in refusal. The Asian slightly shook his turbaned head and took Frankie gently by the arm: the gesture was sufficiently respectful, and they set off together in silence. Round two and a half corners they went into a Pakistani café with a smell of stale spices, a juke-box, a broken fruit-machine, and several English girls.

MR JUSTICE

By Latimer road, Pc Edward Justice went into the London Transport gents: not for that purpose, nor (since he was uniformed) to trap some evil-doer, but simply to change his socks round from foot to foot. As he did so, balancing carefully on some sheets of tissue he'd laid out on the stone, he read the obscenities upon the wall. One said,

Man, quite young, nice room, seeks friend for punishment. Please say who and when.

A space was left, and then in capitals:

Men mean a great deal in my life.

Ted Justice took out the pencil from his black official note-book and wrote under the first part,

Blond, 26, and brutal. NAP 1717.

(This was the number of his section-house.) Then, under the second message, he wrote:

Mine too.

He left the establishment with a stern, penetrating glance at those inside it.

In the street and sun he stood, in official posture, before a haberdasher's. In the plate glass he examined himself from helmet tip to boot toe, and up again, adjusted the thin knot of his black tie, and patted his pockets down. All present and correct, sir. What they'd make of the man inside, in a moment, he couldn't tell: but the outward image was immaculate.

He caught the haberdasher's eyes beyond his own, didn't budge or change his expression in the slightest, then moved away, authority incarnate. The socks felt better: but tight and sticky, the serge was hot today. Would he make plain-clothes—*would* he? Think of it! In civvies yet unlike the other millions—up above the law!

'Not now, lady, I wouldn't,' he said to a girl-and-pram combination at a corner and, holding the traffic, he saw her personally across the road. An ugly one, unlike his own, but then for all women he had a quite authentic love: not just the copper's professional solicitude, but a real admiration and affection. Yes: even for women coppers, and some of *them* . . .

He reached the station dead on time, and calm, and spotless. The desk officer looked up and said, 'The Detective-sergeant's ready for you, Ted. Good luck.'

MR LOVE

Of the three girls casually eyeing Frankie and the Asian, one was a short, thick-set chunky woman past her first prime—and second—maybe hitting twenty-eight. Her dark hair was dyed blonde, her face the colour of electric light, and her body desirable in an overall way only (that is, though the immediate impression was attractive, no part of her, on inspection, seemed very beautiful). She spoke less than the others, was very contained and self-assured, yet when she did speak her voice was emphatic and decided. Her clothes accentuated the same features as nature did beneath them, but elsewhere were casual and slack.

After a while of merely glancing at Frank, when he made a sudden movement on his chair she began to watch him. Frankie was used to this and had no vanity about it (though about other things a lot). He knew he wasn't 'handsome' whatever that may mean (for nobody seems to know or to agree), but he also knew he was well set up, and confident, and strong, and potent; and that though he repelled a great many girls for various reasons, for the kind he liked best he'd only to whistle and they'd come. He now whistled by looking steadily at the girl ten seconds in that kind of way.

She got up, came over and holding out a florin, said, 'You got some pieces for the juke?' In reply he took sixpences out of the front pocket of his slacks and, without getting up, stretched over and dropped them in the juke-box. 'What you want?' he asked, still stretching far.

'You choose,' she told him.

'I can't see the names from here,' he said. 'You pick them.'

'I'll press these for you,' she answered, and without taking her finger off the button she moved the selector and jabbed eight times. Then she sat down at the far side of his table.

The juke-box made conversation quite impossible: but as it blared on they spoke to each other, perfectly clearly, with their eyes, their faces, and their limbs. This unspoken conversation established that they liked each other that way, and that way, at the moment, only; and reserved all their lives, and personalities, and friendship, and private particulars to themselves.

When the juke-box stopped neither of them wanted more music, and both looked up with faint resentment for anyone else who might consider feeding it again. The girl put her hands on the table round her bag: a battered, soiled affair, square-black, but efficient and businesslike as a safe is in an office that seems otherwise untidy and impractical. She said to Frankie, 'I'd say you look a bit tired.'

'You would?'

'Yes. Just look it, I mean. That's all.'

'Well, you'd be right. I have been.'

They both ignored the Asian as if he absolutely wasn't there, although at this stage his presence as unconscious chaperon was rather helpful.

'Bad times?' she said.

'Well, girl, you know how it is. No ship—no work—no money.'

'I thought you were one of those,' she said, waited for him to ask her what *she* was, and registered with approval that he didn't.

Now, she played a right card .... but a bit too early. 'Shall we take a walk?' she said.

He paused a fraction more than was usual in a man of quick decisions, and said, 'I'll take a rest here for a while.'

She moved her hands round the bag, didn't hide a slight vexation and said (but quite nicely), 'It was an invitation to you ... You've told me how you're fixed just now ...'

He answered (also without any malice), 'Another time. I won't forget you.'

The girl smiled, took up the bag, said nothing more, and after a few words with the other girls, went out. The Asian was in conversation with a countryman, and Frankie, catching up with this, said to him, 'No, friend, I'll pay ...'

'No, no!' cried the Asian, for the first time in their acquaintance letting drop the smile.

'Let me pay for myself, then,' Frankie Love said, getting up.

'No!' said the Asian, giving money to the Pakistani fiercely.

Frankie now gave him *his* first smile of the day—but a very reluctant, meagre one—and saying no more, shook hands with the Asian, patted his shoulder gently, and went out.

The girl, as he expected, was at the far corner, waiting. As she'd expected, he took his time, and when he came up she made no reference whatever to his change of mind. She shifted her handbag to the other arm, took his, and clicked along the pavement on her stiletto heels.

It was about half a mile. Near the end of the journey, well after she'd passed them, she said of two men standing beside a delivery van, 'Two coppers.'

'Yeah? How you know?'

'You shouldn't look back like that. The way they stared at us.'

'I expect quite a few men stare at you.'

'Not *that* way. It's not sex that interests them ...'

'What does, then?'

She stopped at the door, took a bunch of keys from her bag, looked around, and opened it. 'What I do, does,' she said. 'You coming in?'

MR JUSTICE

THE Detective-sergeant said, 'At ease, constable, have a fag, come and sit down by me.' Ted Justice did so but with caution, mistrusting the affabilities of a superior: for no-one, he'd learned, is kindly without a motive—unless (and even then!) the old-timers who stayed stuck at uniformed sergeant, or below.

'Well, Ted,' the Detective-sergeant said, 'not to beat about the bush at all—you're in.'

'Thank you, sir.'

'In on probation, naturally. We all want to see how you shape up, and keep an eye on you generally.' He stared at Edward in a quite frankly treacherous way. 'So,' he resumed, 'as from tomorrow, civilian dress, please—you'll be drawing the appropriate allowances.'

'Thank you, sir.'

'Stand up, Ted.' Ted Justice did so. 'Take off your tunic and tie.' He hung them neatly on a chair-back. 'Come over in front of this,' and they walked over to the mirror.

Reflected behind him, Edward saw his new superior gazing with him at the mirror's image; and in it his own not very tall, and lean, and wiry and relaxed and sensual body. The Detective-sergeant ruffled Edward's hair, and he didn't flinch. 'Yes, it's extraordinary!' the Detective-sergeant said. 'You don't look like a copper—except, perhaps, for that lovely pair of blue eyes.' He laughed. 'Come and sit down again,' he said. And as Edward moved over, 'Get out of the way of walking like that, please. You're not on the beat any more, remember. It's the first thing that gives the untrained plain-clothes man away.'

'Now,' said the officer, sitting at his desk. 'Forget all you've learned till now. Forget any pals you've made. Here in the vice game, you've moved up a degree.' He paused. 'But: and it's a very important but; though you've moved up above *them*, so far as *we're* concerned you're right down at the bottom once again. I'll be frank with you—you're not a fool. I'm opening a file on you today. If there's anything in that file that we don't like—then out you go, boy! And if you fall, and go back to the beat again, you'll fall even lower than you were before. Agreed?'

'Yes, sir,' said Edward.

'Agreed, then. Now: we're moving you over towards Royal Oak: new section-house, new surroundings. Round here, if you've done your work well, your face is probably a bit too familiar. That's all right? You accept?'

'Yes, sir.'

'Splendid: we want all this to be voluntary. Now, one other thing: and don't take it amiss. In the Force, we don't interfere in an officer's private life as far as is reasonable and possible. But in the CID, we have to. Why aren't you married?'

'Sir?'

'You're not a poof, are you?'

'No, sir.'

'Sure of that?'

'Quite sure, sir.'

'Well?'

Edward thought fast: but knew however fast he thought, the Detective-sergeant would observe it, so he said at once, 'May I ask you one question first, sir?'

'You may. Well?'

'Do I get any expenses?'

The officer looked at him blandly, and with pity. 'I don't like that question very much,' he said. 'To begin with, it's a foolish one. What we're offering you is—well, influence. If you've got any brains, then money's a secondary consideration: or should I say, where there's influence, there's money. Routine expenses can, of course, be recovered: but in this section, frankly, most of us don't bother. How you manage there, provided you keep your nose clean, is really up to you, you know. You understand me, do you?'

'Yes, sir.'

All this, which had entered one corner only of Edward's brain, had given him time to frame his answer. The difficulty was this. He had a girl (in fact a woman, since she was older than himself), and he loved her, and she him, and he had since adolescence loved no other woman in the world or, as it happened, known any other. *But* —and this was it. Her father had been 'in trouble'. And though he was—reluctantly—prepared to bless his daughter's marriage to a copper, the girl herself—who loved the officers now, in the measure

Ted was one—had told him she believed—and she was very lucid on this essential point—that while she would never leave him if he wanted her, to marry him would mean, with absolute certainty, that he'd never rise far in his career: if, indeed, once the Force knew of her, they allowed him to stay in it at all. So what to do? Pretend she did not exist? The uniformed lot might wear that one— but not the sharp boys of the CID: they'd soon discover; for if no one else told them, a nark or a disgruntled criminal would be certain to. Always, Edward had known this was the one chink in his newly burnished professional armour: but loving her so much, he had waited for time, somehow, to resolve the fatal contradiction. What he had *not* foreseen (and was blaming himself for severely at this moment) was that if *he* never spoke about her to the Force, the Force would raise the matter so abruptly.

'I'd like to be frank with you, sir,' he said (determined not to be).

'That's what we want, son. Come on—I'm waiting.'

'I've got a girl . . .'

'Yes . . .'

'But I'm not sure the Force would find her suitable.'

'Why?'

Edward Justice looked his superior officer right in the eyes and said, 'She's one of those persons, sir, who doesn't care for the officers of our Force.'

The Detective-sergeant smiled extremely unpleasantly. 'Doesn't she,' he said. 'She cares for you, I suppose, though.'

'Oh, yes, sir. And on this matter, she may alter. As you can imagine, sir, I've made it . . .'

The Detective-sergeant had got up. 'Shut up,' he said quite gently. 'Look, boy, it's simple. Change her ideas and marry her, or else . . . Well! That quite clear?'

'Of course, sir.'

'Okay. No hurry: but just get it fixed.' He smiled. 'An item for your file,' he added.

Detective-constable Justice put on his tie and jacket. 'Could I ask you, sir,' he said, 'what kind of work you have in mind for me?'

'I don't mind telling you,' the officer answered, taking his trilby hat off a filing cabinet. 'You interested in ponces at all?'

'I'm interested, sir, in whatever you tell me to be.'

'Good. We might try you out with them. What d'you say?'

Edward made no reply, and his senior put his hand on Detective-constable Justice's shoulder. 'Remember one thing,' he said. 'It's the only thing that matters—really.' He looked at Edward like a brother (as Cain, for example, did on Abel). 'Don't ever get in wrong with the Force: because if you do—well, a broken copper's the only person in the world we hate more than a criminal.'

MR LOVE

FRANKIE got up to make two cups of tea, and now for the first time he had a chance of looking round about her room. He liked it. It wasn't rich at all, no; yet as on a ship, nothing essential was missing. The sheets had been clean, and in the tins marked tea, and rice, and sugar, he saw there were actually these things, and plenty. It was, of course, a bit over-feminine, but then the girl was, after all, a woman. 'Sugar?' he said, looking round at her lying smoking on the bed. 'Eight lumps,' she answered. 'I'm not naturally sweet.'

He came and sat beside her and fondled her abstractedly. 'Thanks, girl,' he said. She smiled and said to him. 'There's not many, I can tell you, get a cup of tea as well.'

'I dare say not,' said Frankie.

'*Or* leave as rich as they came in,' she added.

Frankie frowned. 'I've *never* paid for it,' he said, 'and never would, and never will.'

'Oh, I was kidding.' She sipped a bit, and said, 'Not even those geisha girls, you wouldn't?'

'If a girl thinks she wants money from *me*, I'd rather go without.'

'Well, dear, being as you are, I don't expect you've often had to.'

Frankie smiled, then looked at her seriously. 'You like the life?' he said.

'I don't like or dislike, darling: I'm just used to it.'

'Been at it long?'

'Oh, ever since I can remember . . .'

'Yeah—I see. You don't mind if I ask: it doesn't upset you?'

She laughed. 'Upset me? Darling, you can believe me or not, but I just—don't—notice.'

'No? By the way: don't call me "darling", please. I told you my name's Frankie.'

'Yes. Frankie Love. You said so. And you've proved it.'

'But listen. Stop me if I'm curious. When you go out: not knowing who it's going to be. That doesn't disturb you?'

'No.'

'Not at all?'

'No. Only if they're vicious or anything, or try to rob me . . .'

'They try that? That's not right!'

'Sometimes they do . . . But you get to know the types—you'd be surprised.'

'I suppose so.' He took her hands, examined them, kissed them and said, 'But listen. All those men. Maybe two or three a day. Don't you find . . .'

'Two or three? Are you kidding? What you take me for—a mystery?'

'You're mysterious, all right.'

'Not *that* way, I'm not.'

'Yeah. But what I mean is—doesn't it disgust you any? One after another, dozens of them just like that?'

She sat up and fixed the pillows. 'Well, Frankie,' she said. 'First ask yourself this question, please. If you go with me after all those dozens—doesn't it disgust *you*?'

'No. No—but I think that's different.'

'Men do.'

'I suppose so.'

'Look, dear. If you're going into this business at all, it's best to have as many as you can, isn't it? Well, isn't it?'

'I dare say . . .'

'This isn't Mayfair, darling . . .'

'. . . Frankie . . .'

'. . . Sorry. Not Mayfair, but Stepney Green. Seamen and drunks. Thirty bob, a pound—even less, sometimes.'

'But it all adds up.'

'I'll say it does. Pass me that bag.'

'No.'

'Go on!'

'No, I don't want to touch it. I don't like women's bags.'

She jerked her head at him, reached over, and spilled its contents on the bed.

'What's this?' said Frankie. 'Your life's savings?'

'Don't be silly, boy. That's just last night's.'

'You kidding *me* now?'

'Why should I kid you?'

'All that loot?'

'Well, it's not so much ... I pay a Bengali eight a week for this little gaff ...'

'For *this*?'

'Frankie, if you're in business full-time, and your landlord's not ignorant, you don't get a gaff, even down here, for less. And if he *is* ignorant, believe me, it's even worse: he might shop you, or throw you out unexpectedly.'

Frankie gazed at the notes and silver on the blanket. Like money you pick up in the streets, it seemed quite different from the contents of a pay-packet—like valuable stuff that just belonged to *any*body.

'What else you spend it on?' he said.

She looked at him intently, then said, 'Oh, this and that—it soon goes, you know. Expenses are heavy: nylons, for instance. Look! You're not the first who's laddered the best part of a pound ...' She rubbed her leg and said, 'But sometimes there's a bit over and to spare ...'

Frankie reflected. 'Well, I suppose you get your due,' he said. 'It can't be easy ...'

'It's not, Frank, believe me.'

'All the same. Excuse my saying so, but I think a man who *pays* for that's no man at all.'

She got up. 'Oh, I don't think much of them either. But I'm glad there's plenty of them around ...'

'You going?'

'Yes, Frank, I have to. But you can stop here a bit, if you like, till I get back ...'

'You'd trust me alone in here?'

'Yes, of course. What's there to pinch? You don't wear girl's clothes—at least I hope not—and I'm taking this...' And she flourished the square black bag.

Frankie got up too. 'No, I'll be off,' he said.

'Off to where?'

'I'm staying down the Rowton.'

'That sty? I hope it's not given you crabs.'

'Baby, I wash,' he said.

'Me too. Turn the other way, I'm going to before we leave.'

MR JUSTICE

ON his day off, Edward was sitting with his girl in the park at Little Venice, up by the Harrow road. He was proud of his girl because though few men looked at her immediately, once they did so their attention was apt to become transfixed. Their initial disdain was perhaps to be explained by the fact that she wore spectacles, was plump and rather dowdy; but their interest became riveted when they grew aware that she had the tranquillity, the assurance, and the indifference that can denote sexual operators conscious of their powers: aware of them not merely as one woman in competition with all the others (which is only a quarter way to success), but aware of them in themselves absolutely.

He was telling her of his first weeks in the vice game: and these weeks had not been without their tribulations. In the first place, Edward had suffered the humiliation of being himself reported as a suspect by a colleague unaware (or *was* he?) of his real identity as a plain-clothes man. Perhaps this mishap was due to the extraordinary difficulty he found in *loitering* successfully, unobserved. Only a child can rival the absolute right a uniformed officer has, in the public eyes, to linger wherever he wishes. But in plain-clothes... well, what would *you* do if told to watch a house for a couple of hours in a thoroughly inconspicuous fashion? All sorts of stratagems will suggest themselves... but the real art is simply to learn how to loiter as a pastime in itself: just as you are, without disguises; and get away with it. Among adults, Edward noticed, only American servicemen seemed quite naturally to possess this skill.

Then there was the difficulty of moving in the dark. Of course, when in uniform there'd been the manoeuvre of lurking in shop doorways, or in mews turnings. But the whole point in the Force of a uniform had been that people *should* see it, and think twice. Now he'd had to learn to embrace the darkness, to become part of it and use it for himself.

He told some of this in confidence to his girl, but not too much of it because he believed firmly in an ultimate loyalty to the Force so far as its own secrets were concerned; and had learned, in its hard and testing school, that a secret told to *any*one is no longer a secret in any real way at all. Also, he was feeling his way in the new job, and still doubtful and insecure.

'But you like it on the whole,' she said.

'Oh, yes. Who wouldn't.'

'Well, dearest, I *don't*. Oh, don't get me wrong! I mean, only because I seem to see much less of you.'

She moved her head slowly and kissed him, which she did quite un-furtively, warmly and decidedly yet in a private, serious, almost holy way (he thought) that no one in the little park could possibly take except to. He felt together with this short, wonderful embrace, the slight scratch of her spectacles, which enchanted him because of memories.

'I'll tell you one thing,' he said. 'I'm sorry the duties make me see you less because, honest, this new job makes me feel quite a bit lonely.'

'Well, naturally,' she said. 'Any new job does.'

'Not only that.' He hesitated how much to admit because he knew a man who betrays his weaknesses, even to the girl he loves, is giving her weapons for the tenderest blackmail. 'It's like this,' he said. 'The story is all coppers are just civilians like anyone else, living among them, not in barracks like on the Continent, but you and I know that's just a legend for mugs. We *are* cut off: we're *not* like everyone else. Some civilians fear us and play up to us, some dislike us and keep out of our way but no one—well, very few indeed—accepts us as just *ordinary* like them. In one sense, dear, we're like hostile troops occupying an enemy country. And say what you like, at times that makes us lonely.'

She squeezed his arm, said nothing.

'Now in this job the new one, even more so. Because not only the civvies all mistrust you, but—this is what I've discovered—the uniformed men do, too. They're jealous, I dare say, and a bit scared: I've had a few very distant looks from former pals in the past few weeks, I can tell you, and it's not so very pleasant.'

'But there's the satisfaction of your job,' she said, because she knew this was a man's great love by which, if she respected it, she could hold him all the more.

'Oh, yes . . . there's that, of course.'

The time was now approaching, as both knew, when they must have it out about the conflict of love and duty. After a silence made of gathering clouds, she broached the theme and said, 'Did they ask you about me at all?'

'Yes.'

'And what did you tell them?'

Edward was ready, this time, with his answer. He could not, he'd decided, tell her what he'd told the Detective-sergeant: that she was a copper-hater; for then she'd think that, maligning her to his other dearest love, the Force, he'd secretly wished to detach himself from her altogether. Women were so mistrustful! And when you want irreconcilables you have to lie at some point—there's really no other possible solution. So this double betrayal of the Force and her was the price he must pay for the higher idea of love. And he'd made up his mind that he'd say to her what he said now, and that was, 'Darling, I just told them I hadn't got a girl at all.'

She looked him full in the eyes and her own shut, a moment, behind her spectacles; then she said, 'That was probably best: probably the only thing to say.'

'I didn't like it, though.'

She pressed her shoulder closer to him. 'There's only one thing,' she said. 'If my Dad should ever die: have you thought of that?'

'No . . .'

She looked at him. 'In that case, we *could* get married: I mean, there'd be no objection any longer, would there?'

He considered. 'No, I don't think so, but . . . Well, your old Dad's hale and hearty, isn't he?'

'Oh, yes. No. All I meant was we mustn't rule out the possibility of marriage altogether.'

He put his arm round her shoulder. 'I should think not! And there's also this. When I get on in the CID, get influence and get to know the men up at the top, the whole position—about you, I mean—might be reconsidered. Specially if your Dad goes on keeping out of trouble.'

'Yes. Well, he has done, hasn't he, for quite a while ... I've seen to that ...'

'I do wish I could offer you marriage!' he exclaimed. 'Here and now! Right out in the open.'

'Well, Ted, we've had that out a thousand times, and you know I've said I understand and it's quite all right with me ... It's you I want, not your name. And my money's good so we've no economic worries, and I'll just put up with it and hope. It's all thought out and decided ... But there is just one thing: what if we had a baby?'

'We won't! You don't mean that you're ...'

'No, no. But what if we *did*? It can happen. And honest, Ted, though you know I'd love and cherish it, I don't want to make your son and mine illegitimate.'

He laughed nervously and a bit crudely. 'Let's face that problem,' he said, 'if it arises. And let's hope it doesn't arise at all.'

She hid her feelings about this (which were multiple, and would have amazed and alarmed Edward considerably) and only said to him, 'I don't mind being your mistress, Ted, but not having a baby makes me feel just a bit like a whore.'

'Eh? Them? Don't talk daft. Anyway, some of them have babies, I can tell you.'

'On purpose? Do they mean to?'

'Some do, I suppose ... They're women, after all ...'

'You're seeing them, then, in your new job?'

Edward grew just a bit portentous. 'Actually, yes,' he said, 'it is concerned with those matters—but more so with their ponces.'

'Oh, yes. They've all got them, have they, these women?'

'Not all: no, not by any means all. The older more experienced type of girl does without, but not the majority, I'd say. They seem to need them.'

'And what are they like, those men?'

'Which? The ponces? Well, that darling's what I'm wising myself up on. It seems they're *all* types. I've had one or two pointed out that between you and me, if the vice boys hadn't assured me of it, I'd just have taken for—well, for anyone in this park.' He gazed at the inoffensive ramblers. 'But then, you see,' he continued, 'that's one of the very first things they teach you in the Force: that every-one—repeat, *every*one—however innocent-seeming, is a potential suspect.'

She gazed at the park population too. 'And how do you catch them?' she asked.

He looked round, lowered his voice and said, 'Well, that's tricky, it appears: you wouldn't think so, but it's very tricky. Because you've got to prove several quite different things. Number one, that the girl's a known and habitual common prostitute. Number two, that she's earned all her money—or the bulk of it—from prostitution. Number three—that the money she earns this way she hands over to him—and that *he* hasn't got any other principal visible means of support.'

'I see,' she said.

'It's more than I do, believe me. There's one thing they always slip up on, though, so I'm told. If you can get the *woman* to testify against him—then you've got him! And as women have all sorts of reasons for losing interest in their fancy-man—well, dear, I leave it to your imagination!'

She shook her head and said, without condemnation, 'I think it's horrible.'

He paused, then answered, 'Well, as a matter of fact I think it is as well. Not, mind you, that I'm setting myself up as a judge: that's not *our* part of the little business; and one of the very first things we learn is not to condemn and simply to detect. But after all: even allowing for that, these ponces are doing something rather special that puts them in a class apart. I'd say they're making money out of love—or out of sex, at any rate. And personally, darling, I consider love is sacred: the one and only really sacred thing that's left: and if you make money out of *that*, then you're destructive and should be destroyed.'

MR LOVE

FRANKIE LOVE and the girl sat in a café (known to the local girls as 'judge's chambers') waiting for the arrival of the solicitor's clerk. 'Now, I don't know,' Frankie said, 'why you want to mix *me* up in all your bits of trouble.'

'Trouble? It's not trouble! Anyway, you're my friend, aren't you?'

'I'm your friend, yes, but until I get a ship or even a job I want to keep clear of law, and courts, and solicitors—the lot.'

She laughed. 'Oh, don't be so silly, Frankie! This isn't *trouble*! A soliciting charge? I've had dozens of them.'

'Then what you want me here for?'

She looked at him seriously. 'Well, Frank,' she said, 'this *is* a bit different as a matter of fact: it is a bit dodgy, and I felt the need of a pal around to give me courage.'

'Courage to do what?'

'Well, I'm not pleading guilty this time for once.'

'You usually do?'

'Always. In the first place I almost always *am*, in the second, what can you do with magistrates against copper's evidence? and in the third—well, if you plead not guilty it's a fiver instead of forty bob: or if the charge was hotted up to something worse, he might even send you to the Sessions.'

'Who might? What Sessions?'

'The magistrate. And if he did the law would have a barrister, and juries just don't like whores—however often some of them have had a go with one of us.'

'Why you taking a chance, then?'

'Well—just because I'm sick of it!'

'Of what?'

'I'll tell you. There's a young fellow—vice-squad copper—who's always asking me to take him home for free. Well, some of the girls do that—but I just won't: not if I don't *like* the feller, anyway. Last time he said, "Do what I say, or else." And this is the "or else": he's bringing a charge.'

'The bastard!' Frankie cried, genuinely revolted. 'That's not right!'

'I don't think so either.'

Frankie pondered. 'But he'll get you all the same, from what you say.'

The girl looked round the café and said gently, 'Perhaps not, you know—it all depends on the date of the alleged offence the charge is for.'

'How come?'

'Well, I've been having my whatsits this last week. With some of the girls that makes no difference—they just ram in some cotton wool and soldier on. But me, no, I'm particular: I stay at home those days—of which fact I've got witnesses.'

'But baby—he's not a mug. He won't bring a charge unless he saw you at it, will he?'

She stared at him, amused. 'Boy, are you crazy? He wouldn't even bother to leave his desk! He'd make the charge blind. Against a known and convicted common prostitute? It's a pushover!'

'Unless you can prove . . .'

'That's it: an alibi.'

'I see.'

'You do? Smart boy! Here comes the shark from the solicitor's.'

With a cheery wave and a cry of 'How do, girl!' there now approached a tall, mackintoshed, somewhat lumbering young man with dark greased hair and a sharp but uncritical regard. He sat at their table, said, 'How do?' to Frankie without asking who he was, and called out for a cup of tea and a cheese roll.

'Money, money,' he said cheerfully, holding out his hand. 'The old firm doesn't even move without a sub.'

From the black bag the girl handed him some notes which he counted, folded each one of them singly, and stuffed in a hip pocket, saying, 'Ta very much, dear.'

'It's we who keep your wife and kids for you,' the girl told him.

'Don't I know it! And the magistrates'! Have you ever thought of that? What wouldn't the courts cost the poor old taxpayers if it wasn't for all you girls and the thousands of forty bobs your little cases attract?'

'Let's talk business, son,' the girl said. 'We'll be on very soon.'

He shifted his glasses on his nose and said, 'Well, I know you girls *never* want to hear advice, which is all we're really useful for, however, mine is—let's get it over—please dear, plead guilty.'

'You know why I'm not.'

'Oh, I do! And I understand your feelings! But do you *really* want to take the law on single-handed? Do just think a bit of the consequences!'

The girl frowned. 'Not the law, stupid—only this one feller.'

The clerk looked at her. 'I'm surprised at you,' he said. 'Look! The law may have their internal wrangles and suspicions, and all be ready to shop one another if it means promotions. But to the outside world—and particularly, excuse me being frank, a girl like you—it's one for all and all for one, they live or hang together.'

'I think he's right,' said Frankie.

'You do? What do *you* know about it?' she cried.

Frankie got up. 'I'll be seeing you,' he said. 'It's none of my business anyway.'

She grabbed him by the seat of his slacks and yanked him down. 'Don't go,' she said. 'I'm sorry—I'm wrought up. I always am a bit just after my monthlies.'

There was a pause. Then the lawyer said, 'Look dear, there's another aspect. He might have brought this not to get his vengeance or anything like that, but just because he wanted a little birthday present.'

'You think so?'

'Well, it's possible, isn't it? Vice-squad boy? Now, if that's so . . . I shouldn't tell you this, my gov'nor wouldn't like it . . . why don't you settle with him? After all: even if you plead guilty it's forty bob, and if you don't there's us to pay as well in addition to all that might happen up at the Sessions if he brought in a brothel-keeping charge or something.'

'They take bribes?' said Frankie.

'Oh, don't be silly!' the girl answered.

The lawyer gave Frankie a rather puzzled look. 'Well, naturally,' he said. 'Imagine yourself please, for a moment, in their position. Girls sitting on a gold-mine, you've got complete powers of arrest, and the courts believe your word, not theirs. Your wages are maybe twelve or so a week. What would *you* do?'

'I wouldn't bring false charges,' Frankie said. 'I don't say I'd be all that particular about everything, but I couldn't bring false charges.'

The lawyer smiled slightly, and the girl was still silent. Then the lawyer said, 'Would you like me to see this feller for you?'

'Isn't it too late?' she asked.

'Oh, to withdraw the charge, it is. But not how it's pressed ... there's evidence and evidence, you know.'

The girl, suddenly, slammed her bag on the formica table. 'You're all a bunch of sharks!' she cried. 'I'll plead guilty—give me back my money!'

'Now, don't be silly,' said the lawyer, his glasses almost falling off his nose in his surprise. 'You've got me down here, and you've asked me my advice ...'

'You'd better give it back,' said Frankie.

The lawyer turned on Frankie Love, completely unimpressed. 'Now *please*,' he said. 'Don't *you* join it.'

The girl put her hand on Frankie's arm. 'He's right, dear,' she said. 'I was a bit vexed, that's all'—and she got up.

'So you won't be needing me in there,' the lawyer said, preparing to rise too. 'If you're going to plead guilty it's best for you there's no defence forces whatever to be seen.'

'I know,' she said. 'But stick around, will you, in case there are complications.'

The lawyer nodded, and called for another tea and roll. Frankie said to her, 'You want me to come with you?'

'Oh no, dear. But mind this for me, will you? They don't like to see that we're not destitute in there.' And she walked out leaving her bag beside Frankie on the table.

Gingerly, he put it on the seat beside him, the lawyer watching casually. Then Frankie said, 'Apologies for speaking out of turn just now.'

'Oh, quite okay! I know how you feel about all this.'

'How *I* feel?'

'Well—yes,' said the clerk, retreating slightly behind his spectacles and munching the second cheese roll. 'I hope she'll not be long,' he added. 'It all depends where her name is on the list.'

'You handle a lot of these cases?'

'Hundreds. And I mean hundreds. My gov'nor deals in vice business almost exclusively, and we're greatly in demand. And though everyone believes we're scoundrels (which of course we are

—har-har), we do have our uses because, believe me, without a lawyer you're just a dead duck in advance. With us to help you, you only lose a leg or maybe, if you're fortunate, a few tail feathers.'

'What: you work chiefly for these girls?'

'By no means! Very rarely, in fact—their cases are usually so simple. No. For the vice barons: the gaff landlords and the escort-businesses that handle call-girls and, of course . . .' the lawyer dropped his eyes '. . . the easy-money boys, the ponces.'

'Those bastards.'

The clerk looked up sharply. 'Yes, those ones,' he said.

Frankie Love had his hand resting on the girl's bag. Suddenly, the penny dropped.

'Here!' he cried. 'You think *I'm* one? *Me?*'

'Well, son—aren't you?'

Frankie raised his fist and cried, 'You dirty little lump of shit!'

The lawyer shot back his chair two feet without rising, looked quickly round the café and said, 'Well, excuse me, *aren't* you?'

Frankie was impressed by the total sincerity of the lawyer's complete surprise. He lowered his fist and said, 'Well, I'll be buggered! Do I look like one?'

The clerk carefully adjusted his seat and picked up his tea again. 'Boy!' he said, 'who *does?* Just do me a favour, will you? Just attend the courts for a week and *look* at them. Except for the odd exception, they all look exactly . . . well, like you and me or anyone at all.'

Frankie laughed. 'Well, I'll be fucked!' he said. 'Just fancy that!'

'You use a lot of bad language, son,' the lawyer said.

'Excuse me again: I didn't mean it.'

The lawyer said, 'Forgotten—excuse *me*, too.' He paused. 'What is your profession, then, if I might ask?'

'Seaman.'

'Seaman. Got a ship?'

'No.'

'Got some other job?'

'No. Not yet.'

'Pardon this question: please don't take it amiss: you ever taken money from that girl?'

There was quite a wait, and for the first time in many years, Frankie blushed. 'I *have* borrowed a few quid from her,' he said.

'*Borrowed.*'

'That's what I told you.'

'All right—all right. Don't hang me, sailor.' The clerk stirred his cup thoughtfully, then said, 'I'm going to tell you something if you want to hear it, but on two conditions. The first is you don't hit me, please. The second is you don't tell the girl because, after all, she's supposed to be my client. Do you agree?'

'Go on . . .'

'You seem a nice boy, and I think I ought to tell you. So here it is. If a vice copper saw you near the courts with a woman coming up on a soliciting charge, and waiting in a caff holding her bag while she went in, and he knew you'd had money from her, and he knew you'd got no job, he wouldn't *ask* you if you are a ponce, believe you me! He'd know you *were* one, and a bloody foolish one at that!'

Frankie Love looked at him steadily, then rose and said, 'Thanks. Would you do something for me, please? Give her this bag. And tell her if she comes near me again I'll crunch her.'

MR JUSTICE

'To show you the ropes,' the Detective-sergeant had said, 'I'll have you go around a while with our star sleuth, as we all call him. He's a young feller just about your age, a bit too big in his boots for a detective-constable, and chances his arm rather more than I think is wise even in our little line of business. But he's a good lad basically, and he certainly gets results. Don't make the mistake, though, of thinking you can get away with everything he does.'

The star sleuth fascinated Edward: he was born to his function like a thoroughbred to the turf, and although so young seemed to know intimately, by instinct, how the whole machinery of the Force could be made to function. During his military service, Edward had noticed the same thing in some young soldiers: there were recruits of only a fortnight who—except for certain gaps of experience, easily corrected—instinctively *knew* how the whole army functioned: what were the real rules behind Queen's Regulations, what duties you could ignore, what prohibited manoeuvres you could safely undertake. In appearance the star sleuth was remarkably nondescript (yet another advantage, Edward reflected!) but not, as he soon discovered, in character or skill.

On their first day out together the star sleuth said, 'Well, I've nothing on, let's just take a walk around.' The tone, scarcely disguised, suggested that he had a lot 'on', and considered Edward's company an imposition. As they walked round the streets between the Harrow road and the railway to the West, his companion said absolutely nothing: being one of those rare men who do not feel the nervous urge to talk so as to establish their identity, and who can remain silent without positively appearing to be rude.

Finding this unbearable, Edward commented on it: 'You're a man of few words,' he said, after fifteen minutes of none whatever.

The star sleuth looked sideways as he walked. 'I can talk quite a bit when necessary,' he said.

'Oh, I believe you,' Edward answered.

'I'll tell you something, boy,' the star sleuth said, stopping at the end of a short road leading to a brick precipice that overhung the railway lines below. 'I'm not here to *teach* you. As a matter of fact I'll be frank with you, I'm still learning as well and what I discover I like to keep strictly to myself. But: here's one tip: *learn* to be silent.'

'Not shoot off your mouth, you mean? Well, obviously.'

The star sleuth folded his arms upon the wall. 'More than that,' he said. 'Look! Suppose you've knocked off a suspect. What do you want to make him do? Talk, isn't it? Well—and believe me. The best way to do it—and the quickest and the *kindest* (he grimaced)—is to say not a word to him yourself. Not a bloody word. Make him wait, say nothing, just come in and *look* at him occasionally. If there's one thing most human beings just can't bear—particularly when they're sitting in the station—that thing is silence.'

'Sometimes you have to talk to them, don't you?'

'Why?'

'Well! Well—suppose it's not a suspect, but a nark or someone who's come to give you information.'

'Exactly the same!'

'Yes?'

'Yes! I'm telling you. Silence.'

'Why?'

'Oh—why? You want me to tell you *why*? Well, that's a bit hard until you've had the experience yourself. But try to get hold of this one.' The star sleuth stuttered slightly, as if wresting a secret from his breast. '*All* men and women you meet professionally are criminals.'

'*Every* one?'

'All. If you want to get anywhere you've got to treat everyone as such.'

Edward digested this as, below his eyes, the Plymouth Belle racketed by. 'That's going a bit far,' he said.

'Is it? Well, you know best. Wait and see.'

'You mean ... Say someone comes in to report he's found a bicycle. You suspect him?'

'Of course. He's number one on my list.'

'It's a thought ...' said Edward.

The star sleuth dusted his arms, and turned round to lean in the sun with his back against the wall.

'If you start with that principle,' he said, 'you really can't go wrong. And if you stick to it and are true to it, it will automatically stop you making a lot of other silly beginner's mistakes.'

'Such as what?' said Edward. 'I'm listening ...'

'I hope so—because sonny, frankly, I don't want to waste all this if it's going to be wasted on *you*. Here are some golden rules, then: get out your note-book and write them down if you feel like it. (The star sleuth chortled.) First is—never go to them: make them come to you.'

'Who?'

'Anyone. It's just like football, boxing, bull-fighting—anything. Make them come to you and then you've got them.'

'And if you can't?'

'You're no damn good. Next, never let them get the impression they're doing the law a favour. Now, suppose someone walks out of that slum there—comes running over—"Officer, I've found a corpse!" —this is your big opportunity for a case ... don't thank him, don't even *answer*, just make him feel he's done what he's *got* to do.'

'Yes, that seems sound.'

'Oh, *thank* you! Now, number three—and that'll do for today, I think—*never* answer questions: always ask them.'

'Oh, I know that one . . .'

'*Do* you? All right. I'm a dear old lady, I come up and say to you, "Constable, can you tell me the way to the Town Hall?"—what do you say?'

'Don't I tell her?'

'Oh—of course! But first you say, "Is it the sanitation department you need, madam, or the rates?" See? Put them on the defensive—always.'

'Oh. I get it.'

'No, you don't—you've forgotten something.'

'*I* have?'

'Yes. What else do you say to her?'

'Well—tell me.'

'You say, "By the way, madam, it's more usual these days to say 'officer', not 'constable'." '

'Correct, yes, I'd say that.'

'So there it is. All in a nutshell. Very simple!'

Without warning, the star sleuth started back up the road again. Edward Justice fell in by his side and said, 'I think some of what you tell me would surprise the old Detective-sergeant just a little.'

The star sleuth stopped. 'Oh *him*,' he said. 'What does *he* know? He belongs to the generation of Pc 49: crafty and tough and not a brain in his thick head.'

'Take it easy, mate.'

'I do, constable!'

They started off again. Ted Justice felt the conversation was now closed, but he had one final question. 'All you said about *every*one being criminal,' he asked. 'Does that apply to us as well?'

'Naturally.'

'To you and me and the Detective-sergeant?'

'Yes.'

'You don't even trust your colleagues in the Force, then?'

'Colleagues! I trust them for one thing, and one only. There are exceptions—but in a fight they're brave and they're reliable. Alone in a dark lane with a bunch of Teds they won't stab you in the back —no, they'll help you come what may. But otherwise . . .'

His voice and his whole posture and expression showed Edward clearly that the shutters were now down, and should not be prised open any more.

Out in the Harrow road the star sleuth stopped to gaze around the vital, squalid thoroughfare, and stood as if sniffing the breeze on a safari. Then he walked half a block, went into a tobacconist's, bought a packet of Senior Service and paused, undoing it, beside the notice-board outside.

On this were handwritten advertisements, some apparently of great antiquity, which mostly offered lodgings with innumerable restrictions. Other invited the purchase of items which no one (except, perhaps, a film studio shooting a Dickens story) would dream of buying. A third category, sometimes with crude photographs, advertised 'models'. The star sleuth scanned these, then withdrew a bit with Edward Justice.

'Whores, I suppose,' said Edward.

'The strange thing is though, boy, that quite a lot of them actually *are* models. In this fair land of ours there's loads of kinky characters who just like sitting and *gazing* at a chick's tits for a couple of quid. Please don't ask me why.'

'And that's quite legal?'

'More or less, it is.'

'But some of them *are* prostitutes?'

'Of course. Nothing illegal about that, either. Under the new act they mustn't solicit in the streets, and if there's more than one of them it's a brothel. Otherwise . . . it's just a business: and believe me, half the time we're called into protect *them*.'

'From the ponces?'

'Not usually . . . In the first place, a ponce with any sense won't live with his girl: they've two addresses, like any other business couple. And in the second—well frankly, most of the stories you hear about brutal bullies putting innocent teenagers on the streets are crap.'

'But that does happen?'

'Oh, yes. With young, or mental, or maybe masochistic girls. Most of the girls are tough and quite intelligent, though. They have to be. And girls of that type simply wouldn't wear it.'

'But the men *do* thump them . . .'

'Oh, frequently! But that's part of the kick: it's all for love!'

The star sleuth took Edward's arm and said, 'As we pass again, just take a look at the bottom left-hand corner one.'

Ted did, and he read:

BETTINA
Is a Continental girl
and very serious. All
poses by appointment.
VEN 5121.

Further along, the star sleuth said to Edward, 'Well?'

'I'd say she's one.'

'Of course! But what sort of one?'

Go on . . . Don't tease me, I'm very willing to learn . . .

'Well. "Continental" doesn't mean she *is*, but what she'll *do*. "All poses" rams the point home and "by appointment" says you can tell her what, over the blower, to see if your kinks match up. "Very serious", of course, suggests the sexual slant in this particular case. New Olympia typewriter with a clean ribbon, so she's possibly expensive.'

'In this area?'

'Why not? Where whores are concerned there *is* no fashionable section if she's good—I mean for where her gaff actually is. Anyway, kinky clients like a slum, and respectable gents prefer an area where they'll not be known.'

'The notice cost her much?'

'Pound a week, unless the tobacconist's an imbecile. For honest landladies, only 2s 6d or something similar.'

'But, tell me. Doesn't advertising like that put us on to her?'

'Why not? It's legal: and even if not, it'd take every cop in London to trace all the notices on boards . . . Besides: put yourself in the poor girl's place. The new laws make it difficult for them on the streets: so how *do* they contact their clients—tell me that, please?'

'No, you go on . . .'

'Well: best is, take a chance and go on the streets three months or so, and build up a clientele.'

'And give them the phone number.'

'Clever boy—exactly. Then, as we know, there's the notice-board technique. Another one: a good contact in the drinking-clubs or all-night garages: barman, doorman, owner, anybody.'

'These pimps take a cut?'

'Don't waste my time! Then there's the escort-businesses—know about them? No? All right: you're a wool-grower from New Zealand, shall we say. You want to meet a nice friendly young lady for a sociable evening out. You're with me?'

'That's legal too?'

'Who for, the agencies? Well, lots of the dates they make are kosher. But several of these agents *have* gone inside on procuring charges...'

'What about Madams?'

'Ah! Yes, there are those: and respectable clients actually like to deal with them because though it costs five times as much, she irons out all the awkward creases for them. Failing the Madams, a new mystery can also find a successful call-girl who'll sub-let clients to her at a percentage.'

Edward laughed. 'We do make it difficult in this country, don't we!' he said.

'That's probably half the charm: the mugs like it to be awkward and mysterious—but not, of course, too dangerous for them.'

'So the new laws have made the whole thing harder.'

'Not really. No, I wouldn't say so. Who they've made it harder for are stupid girls and semi-pros who've been knocked out of business because they can't use the streets any longer. The clever ones have just gone on the phone. And here's a funny thing: once they're established with their clients, it's actually *easier* for them.'

'It is?'

'Well yes, it is. Take gaffs. A crooked gaff with the landlord in the know cost forty a week at least with maybe key money in decent areas—when you could get them. That was for street girls. But once you're on the phone, you can get a straight place just like anyone else for ten a week or so. Of course, if the caretaker or some friendly neighbour rumbles you—out you go! But you'd really be surprised, if the girl's discreet and chooses her clients carefully, how *little* people notice. You see: English people are nosy, sure enough, as we all know; but they've also got a great thing about minding their own business. That's very valuable to the girls. So with the new laws I'd say this: there'll be just as much vice, just as many millions spent on it, but fewer women. Conclusion: profits per head—or tail—will rise. That's all.'

Edward was overwhelmed by this expertise: and, like an anxious angler, handled his companion with the utmost care lest an inappropriate reaction or remark might plunge him back into taciturnity. With prudence, though, there seemed little danger of this: like many silent men the star sleuth, once started, was a chatterbox, and opinionated (not without reason), and something of a fanatic: which the speed and urgency of his narrow voice conveyed vividly to Edward as they walked on along the Harrow road.

'And what,' Edward asked, 'about the ponces?'

'Those bastards,' said the officer, stopping by the canal bridge.

'Yes. How do they fit in?'

'They come out best of all,' the star sleuth said.

'With the new laws?'

'Yes.'

'Why?'

'Like this,' said the star sleuth, peering at the cats and contraceptives floating on the Grand Union canal. 'You're a ponce—right! Your girl is on the streets—yes? Well, if she is she's certainly had several convictions. But if she's a call-girl—particularly if she's started out as one without going on the streets at all—there's quite likely nothing known against her: no convictions, anyway. Very well. Try proving to a magistrate—let alone a jury—that the male companion of an innocent, unconvicted woman is living off her immoral earnings!'

'So what can you do about them?'

'We're working out techniques to meet the situation. The best is, opinion seems to be, to raid her premises with a warrant for suspected brothel-keeping and sweep him into the net, somehow, in the process. Then, once you've got him, a little chat will probably produce results. That is, if you can *find* him: because the craftier among the ponces are naturally very elusive. And if their woman's loyal to them it's going to be tricky in the extreme.' The star sleuth took out a halfpenny and dropped it in the canal. 'But not impossible,' he added.

MR LOVE

FRANKIE had paid his last visit to the Labour because he'd told the clerks there, without venom but with extreme precision and contempt, that he wasn't going through the comedy of 'signing on' any more just like a schoolboy, and that it was *their* job to get him a ship and if they couldn't, well then, fuck them. They'd said—also without malice but with all the equal contempt of the employed official for the jobless—that that was up to him, here was his week's money and if he didn't want any more then of course he needn't bother to sign on. With these few pounds Frankie went down among the seamen's homes of Stepney to try to arrange to stow away: not on a long trip, he was not so daft as that, but just to another port where the proportion of mariners to landsmen might be more favourable to his hopes and mental comfort.

On his way down by Leman Street, on the other side of the road, approaching him, he saw the girl: and walked straight ahead, ignoring her; but as they passed his eyes pulled his head round . . . and he saw it wasn't she but just another: and as soon as he knew it wasn't, wished it had been.

Like children (and most men), Frankie was attracted by what, for reasons of pride more than real inclination, he had rejected. The episode near the courts had left him speculating—naturally—on what, if he *had* been her ponce, the life would have been like: and as with so many of us, what we have speculated on at length becomes with time the thing we mean to do. A few weeks' reflection, too, had taught him that essentially the girl, by her oblique and crafty offer, hadn't really meant him any harm: her manoeuvre had in its way been flattering; and also—for Frankie was unusually free from self-delusion—had been one that, things being as they were, might as well be rationally considered.

The chief—in fact, the only real—reason against it all was that Frankie thought ponces were bums, and seamen princes. But suppose you were a prince without a throne? That it was criminal didn't worry him particularly, since Frankie's code of honour (which most certainly existed) at times coincided with, but at times departed completely from those enshrined by any established sets of laws. For example: he wouldn't hesitate a second to wound a man—or even, if it came to that, to kill him—if it was to help a friend—a rare and real one. And as for the sexual aspect, this didn't worry him at all: because for Frankie, sex *was* love; and sexual attachment the only profound relationship with a woman that he considered possible. The money, of course, would be—well, obviously—useful. Like many seamen, Frankie wasn't greedy about money and only felt the urgent need of it for explosive blow-outs when ashore in port. On board—with food and a berth and working clothes—he felt no need of it at all and even forgot at times, completely, how much back pay the company might owe him. But to be *destitute*: and on land! That was a real horror, a most shameful and miserable misfortune.

So—all things considered—hadn't he been a fool to turn her down so finally and abruptly? Quite clearly, poncing would be dangerous . . . you'd need to find out a lot more about the tackle and ropes of *that*. As obviously, a great deal would depend on how far you could trust the woman; and—more to the point—dominate her. Because in Frankie's sharp and hard experience a woman, like a ship, was reliable only if you had her under strict and complete control.

Nevertheless: the sea, certainly, came first—and far away so—if it would have him back. No woman and no fortune would hold him from that great and utterly dependable she. So, filled with the determination of a wise and right decision, he spent an energetic day among the nautical layabouts of Wapping. But though he drank a very great deal—and they—no one, apparently, could fix anything or even make a practical suggestion. And as night fell he grew not just dejected and intoxicated, but—worst of all for a man whose mind and spirit waxed and waned in power with the strength of his animal energy—he grew spiteful, tired and angry. 'Oh, well,' he said, 'anything rather than the Labour'—and he set off on foot to her address.

Repeated ringing brought no answer: till he became aware from the movement of a curtain that there was someone up there. He withdrew ostentatiously; returned and waited a whole hour in a near-by doorway (fortifying himself from a hip flask) and then, when another lodger entered, ran up and got his foot inside the door.

This man (in fact, the landlord) vigorously protested, but Frankie simply lifted him up and placed him on one side, walked up the stairs, banged on the door, heard angry shouts, heaved against it several times and broke inside. The girl was standing by the table holding a breadknife, and her companion, a short, dark man, remained sitting watchfully beside his loaded plate.

'Get out!' the girl cried.

'Not me,' said Frankie '—him.'

'You're drunk!' she shouted.

'Of course. Is he a customer? Tell him to go!'

'He's not. He's what *you* were too bloody high-and-mighty to want to be.'

And now the man made a rush. Frankie was used to the Maltese, and didn't underestimate them at all. They're fast, fearless, and mean business, he knew. He raised a whole leg quickly and braced himself against the wall: the Malt ran into it and lost his knife. Unfortunately for him his shoes were off his feet, and Frankie (recalling an episode in Williamstown, Victoria) had gone for both of them with all his eleven stone while keeping a fraction of a weather eye on the girl and, more particularly, her breadknife. But she didn't use it or move, and the Maltese was in agony. Frankie kicked him again, ripped his slacks down by a swift tear at his belt (another Victorian expedient), then closed in, heaved him to the open door and literally 'threw him down the stairs'.

The girl ran out and cried, 'Give him his coat here or he'll call the law!'

Frankie threw it down after him. 'You want me call the law?' the Bengali landlord echoed.

'No, no—I'll see you straight: a fiver!' cried the girl.

The front door slammed on the Maltese. They went back in the room. 'Well!' said the girl. 'You *are* a lively boy!' He grabbed her and got to work ferociously.

An hour or so later they sorted themselves out and resumed the meal abandoned by the Malt. She was gazing at him with frank admiration and also (but perhaps he missed this) with a triumphant, proprietory glint. Downing his VP wine, he said to her, 'Hand me that thing.'

'My bag?'

'You heard.'

She passed it over with a smile and he upended it. 'Not much,' he said.

'Others have been at it.'

'Not any more.'

'No? Hi! You're not going to be one of *those*, are you?' she cried as she saw him stuffing all the notes into his slacks pocket.

'One of what?'

'One who takes *every*thing.'

'Why—is this all you've got?'

'Sure.'

'Don't kid me!'

'Darling, why should I? You'll soon find out.'

'Nothing hidden?'

'*Hidden?* Are you crazy? In this dump? My bag's the only safe place—it never leaves me.'

He put it down. 'Haven't you got any savings?' he asked her.

'*Savings?* Darling! What you take me for!'

'Well—we're going to change all that; we're going to save.'

'Are we? Well, dear, I'm all for it—but it's going to be up to you.'

'Okay. I'll see to it.'

'Nice of you. Meantime, could I have a couple of quid for pin money? Only two . . .'

'Of course.'

'*Thank* you. You *are* good to me!'

He kissed her and upset some crockery. She disentangled. 'And will you tell me,' she said, 'just *how* you're going to save this money?'

'*How?* Put it in the bank.'

'Oh, yes? The GPO? The Midland?'

'Well—why not?'

She looked at him. 'Darling,' she said, 'I love you, but honest, you worry me, you've got a *lot* to learn.'

'Well—teach me.'

'Suppose you're nicked—just on suspicion. And they find you've got a bank account. What then?'

'I see.'

'You do? Well, then. What next?'

'We'll put it in your name.'

'Oh! So you trust me! Suppose I walk out on you?'

'You won't.'

'Won't I? Dear, in this business you just *never* can tell.'

She got up, picked up her chair and came round and sat beside him. 'Listen,' she said. 'Let's get a few things straight. I love you, Frankie, but there'll be rows enough if I know you—and know me—and there's some we can skip by right from the start avoiding misunderstandings.'

He lit a fag. 'Okay,' he said. 'I'm new on board. Please clue me up.'

She was looking at him again. 'You know,' she said, 'before we think of anything like saving, we *must* get you a new suit.'

'Oh, that can wait.'

'And shirts and shoes and spare slacks and things.'

'Come on—get on with it. Lay down the cards.'

'Very well, then. And let's have first things first. I *don't* want a ponce who isn't faithful.'

'Why shouldn't I be?'

'That's what they all say! But please understand this, Frankie, very clearly. If you want to mess around with any other girl, do please just tell me and we'll wind it up. But don't try to deceive me.'

'That seems right enough to me. And what about you?'

'Me?'

'You and any other men.'

'I hope you don't mean the customers ... because, darling, they just mean sweet fuck-all to me.'

'But what if one ever did?'

'I'd not see him again.'

'You promise?'

'I'm not the sort of girl who has to *promise*. If I say so, it is so.'

'Me, too. All right, then. What else?'

'I want to change my business completely. I want a big change in my whole life. I want to go on the phone.'

'Like call-girl?'

'Oh, Frankie! Your knowledge, boy!'

'I'm a seaman, do remember. I've got stacks of foreign phone numbers in my diary.'

'Throw it away, then.'

'Okay. So call-girl: why?'

'Because street business is getting too dangerous, because I'm reaching an age when I like to know *who* the client's going to be, and because I'm tired of thirty bobs and call-girl money's better.'

'All right. Will that Asian of yours let you put in your private phone?'

'You crazy, darling? We're moving out! I want to go up West.'

'I've no objection. Any particular area?'

'I thought of Kilburn: it's quiet and quite select.'

'Not too select to get a place, I hope.'

'Baby! This is a straight gaff I'll be looking for—not a crooked one. In fact . . . I've had what I think's quite a bright little idea: try and get a council flat.'

'They wouldn't get to know?'

'Well, if they do—we move. And that brings me to another point. Most of the girls, I don't mind telling you, prefer their boys *not* to have a job so as to make them more dependent. But me, darling, honest, for your own sake I'd rather you had one.'

'I don't mind. If I can get one . . . You know how I've tried . . .'

'Up West, it'll be different and I'll help you. It's protection for you —no need for you to account to anyone for your means of support; and it'd also mean that we could live together.'

'Aren't we going to do that anyway?'

'Oh, of course! But if you *haven't* got a job, it's much safer for you if I live and work in two different places.'

'I get it. All right—find me a job, then.'

She kissed him. He looked up and said, 'Baby, apart from that, what do I have to *do*?'

'Love me.'

'Of course! But nothing else? Don't you need protection or something?'

'Me? Apart from the odd sex maniac I can handle anyone: and even them I can usually spot a mile off. No: all you have to do is be.'

'Okay. But I must say, if you'll not think me ignorant, I don't quite see what *you*'ll get out of it: come to that, what any of you girls do out of having boys.'

She looked at him. 'I'm just wondering,' she said, 'just how much I ought to tell you.'

'It's up to you! This truth thing was your idea anyway.'

'Okey-doke. Well, here it is. Imagine you're a gigolo—right? You hire yourself out to a dozen women a day. How would you feel?'

'Exhausted.'

'No, I mean about your sex life?'

'Disgusted.'

'There you are, then. And wouldn't you feel the need for a real lover—far more than any ordinary woman does?'

Frankie reflected. 'I don't know about that,' he said.

'Well—we do. A ponce, dear, in many cases, is simply an un-married husband. He's our little compensation for the kind of life we lead.'

'All the girls feel that way?'

'Not all—not even all those who *do* have ponces. With some of them it's just to show them off: that they've hooked some splendid great big hunk of man.'

'That's just like *any* girl.'

'A *lot* of things about whores are, dear, as you'll discover.'

'Well—what else?'

'This is the one I shouldn't tell you, but I will. A woman always likes to *own* a man.'

'So you own me?'

'Wait! All women like it. An old bag with a gigolo—doesn't she? A rich wife with a poor husband—doesn't she too? And even respectable women: don't they like to boss their husbands somehow if they can? Get the hooks on them some way? Well, with us it's a mania. And I won't hide it from you, so there'll be no tears, no reproaches. There's *no*body in the whole wide world who's hooked by a woman like a ponce is by a whore.'

'Why?'

'I'll put it to you straight: because he's a criminal and she's not.'

'And she could shop him?'

'Any minute of the day.'

There was silence.

'Yeah,' he said. 'Well, I see that. But it seems to me *he's* not without weapons in his jacket, too.'

'You mean he can bash her?'

'Not only that. If she shops him, when he comes out—if they get him—then he can carve her up.'

'Oh, sure! And it's been done! But darling! She moves first!'

'Or even kill her.'

'Life imprisonment, dear.'

'Also,' he continued, 'just walk out on her.'

'If she doesn't want it?'

'Sure.'

She kissed his hands. 'Well, you know best,' she said, 'and with a nice girl like I am, I don't deny it's true. But if she's a bitch and he says cheerioh, she can make it very, very awkward for him if she wants to.'

Frankie withdrew his hands. 'You know,' he said, 'I'm beginning to wonder what the poor fucking ponce gets out of it at all.'

She laughed. 'Well!' she exclaimed. 'Nice times if she's any good, that others have to pay for. Easy money and a lot of it—a great, great deal. A big boost to his ego—doesn't it make you feel you're like a king? And then, excitement! They do actually love the life, so many of them.'

'Born to it, you'd say.'

'Yes—not like you: you're not the born type, that's why I love you.'

'And have there,' Frankie asked, 'been many others before me in your sweet life?'

'Frank,' she said. 'I'll make a bargain with you. I'll ask you no questions about anything you did before today: if you'll agree to do the same so far as my past life's concerned.'

'Seems reasonable. Okay.' He got to his feet. 'It's lucky for me,' he said, 'that men just can't do without it. None of them.'

She didn't answer that but got up too, and they started to clear the table and wash the dishes together.

'Just one more thing,' she said from among the suds, 'and then my little lecture's ended.' She turned and faced him. '*Do* be careful, please, about the law. Avoid them if you can and don't provoke them. The only good relations a ponce can have with coppers is just none at all.'

'I'm not a dope: I'll remember.'

'It's quite surprising,' she said, 'how much they'll leave you alone, even if they know quite a lot about you, if you keep right clear of them and don't draw their attention to you in any way at all.'

'Okay. I've got nothing against coppers.'

'I'm glad to hear it. A lot of ponces are just copper-haters: and that's so bloody foolish.'

'Hate them?' said Frankie, putting down a china plate. 'Well, me, I don't—why should I? They're part of the system just like ship's officers are—and I never hated them as long as they did their job efficiently and fairly. I didn't even mind unfairness or even a bit of rough-stuff provided they knew how to keep the old ship sailing on. As for the law—well, I've been knocked off once or twice and even bashed up a bit, but I've no real reason to complain. The law's got to be there just like the captain: and I'd say it's got to be respected, even by anyone who chooses to go against it.'

MR JUSTICE

EDWARD's next task was to collect a nark or two: and this was no easy matter. A nark–copper relationship is, in a way, like that of lovers: a particular intimacy that cannot be simply handed over by one officer to another as part of the new officer's inheritance with the files and addresses and card-indexes. A nark must be personally wooed and won: or rather, he and the copper must *discover* each other, just as lovers do, and establish personal ties—the nark offering facts and admiration, the copper small rewards in kind and privilege.

The nark's chief asset in the deal is that really good informers—not so strange as it may seem—are rarer by far than really good coppers are The copper's asset is not, as one might imagine, the meagre advantages which, in reality, he can offer to the nark, but the power and prestige the nark imagines he derives from being attached, though indirectly and informally, to an immensely powerful organization. The nark may be motivated by the love of secrecy (of knowing things that *are* secret from others, however valueless in themselves), and also, it may be, by the almost voluptuous instinct that exists in certain human beings, to betray. There may even (if the nark be intelligent, which he rarely is or he wouldn't be one) exist the deep attraction of an awful fear: of playing with hot and very unpredictable fires. Fear, that is, of the Force and also, even, of what may happen to himself: for sharp narks can hardly fail to perceive how frequently, if they fall foul of an officer or he merely gets tired of them, they themselves are apt to disappear suddenly, unaccountably, inside the nick. But even this does not prevent the really devoted nark from re-assuming, on release, his former role. For narks in their humble way, like the majestic coppers whom they serve, are dedicated souls.

It was a female copper (plain-clothes—and very fetching ones) who gave Edward sound counsel on this point. 'Wait till they come to you,' she said. 'They will.' And sure enough, soon after his first weeks on the job during which he'd had the sensation all the time that dozens of invisible, unidentifiable eyes had been weighing him carefully up, a man approached him by the telephone boxes of Royal Oak tube station (where he was trying to catch a sex maniac whose habit it was to wait till a girl entered the box next to his own, immediately dial *her* number—which he'd previously noted—and when she raised the receiver in astonishment at the quick sound of the bell, utter an obscenity), and the following dialogue took place.

'He's not here today,' the nark said.

'Who isn't?'

'Who you're looking for.'

'Who am I looking for?'

'Madcap Mary.'

'Who's she?'

'He: the feller who makes the calls you're interested in.'

'What makes you think I'm interested in any calls?'

This exchange, to both officer and nark, had already established some essential factors. For all human conversations hold inside and beyond them other, and often larger, conversations that remain unspoken, of which the exchange is just the seventh part (if that's the figure) of the iceberg that breaks surface. Ted knew, for instance, this man knew who he was, what he was after, and something about it. The nark knew he knew all this and that Edward took a lively, but always conditional interest in himself. They'd also assessed quite a bit about each other's characters, and possible utility, and degrees of reliability and of menace. Beyond this there were whole mushroom clouds of supposition, waiting for crystallization in good time.

'I could do with a cup of tea,' the nark said, suddenly feigning a fairly evident mock humility.

Unlike most narks this creature was not small: nor shifty, nor furtive, nor triple-eyed, nor sordid in his attire. He looked like a bus conductor, say, of a suburban line and nearing retirement. They entered the caff separately, then joined up again after getting their two cups, as if casually, at the table near the window.

There was quite a pause, each waiting for the other to begin. The nark, being the older and the more experienced, held out longer, and Edward broke the silence with, 'And how did you know about me?'

'I always do.'

'Always? No one point me out to you?'

'Almost always.'

'How?'

The nark smiled sourly. 'If you could see yourself now,' he said, 'you'd know.'

Vexed, Edward asked him, 'Why?'

'You've got the *double* look.'

'The what?'

'You're wearing it now: watch your pals, you'll get to know it. And then, all coppers *stare*. Nobody else in England, except kids and coppers, *stare*.'

'Go on . . .'

'And then, they listen. Even if you're drunk or bore them stiff, coppers will *listen* to you.'

'But we have to.'

'I'm not saying you don't: only that you do.'

'All right. Anything else?'

'Yes, your shoes. I've never yet seen a cop, even got up as a down-and-out or something, who can bear to be seen around if he's down-at-heel.'

'Really!'

'Yes. And then you don't like running.'

'Come off it! You mean we never chase anyone?'

'Oh, of course you do: but you don't like it.'

'Why would you say we don't?'

'I dunno. Maybe because of those helmets. Even if you're not wearing them you're frightened they'll fall off. Or maybe you just don't like *hurrying*. Or exercise of any kind.'

Edward smiled, quite unpleasantly, too. 'Is that all?' he said.

'There's also your hands.'

'What about them?'

'You're working-men most of you, but you don't like manual labour. That's why quite a lot of you join the Force: to get out of manual labour.'

Edward drained his cup. 'So we're easy to spot,' he said. 'Stick out a mile, you'd say.'

The nark was unabashed. 'Most of you do, yes. That is, except for women coppers. Maybe it's just because they're fewer, or maybe we're all not quite used even now to the idea of them, but—well: even I quite often fail to spot them.'

'Even you.'

'Yes, that's what I said: even me.'

The nark eyed Edward with modest but assured professional pride. 'Don't take it hard,' he said, 'from me. I know you're just starting, and I'm only trying to be of assistance to you.'

'Thank you,' said Edward, meditating in the nark's near future some thoroughly uncomfortable moments.

'The fact is this,' the nark continued, lighting a fag and not offering Edward one. 'You may not approve of what I say, but you and me have one big thing in common: neither of us is mugs: both of us sees below the surface of how things seem.'

'Yeah,' Edward said.

'And I'll tell you something more,' the nark went on. 'It's even the same between you and the criminals, as you'll discover. Neither they nor you belong to the great world of the mugs: you know what I mean: the millions who pay their taxes by the pea-eh-why-ee, read their Sunday papers for the scandals, do their pools on Thursdays, watch the jingles on the telly, travel to and fro to work on tubes and buses in the rush hour, take a fortnight's annual holiday by the sea, and think the world is just like that.'

'I see what you mean,' said Edward Justice.

'Well, now,' said the nark. 'I don't want to waste your time. Are you interested in a little case?'

'I might be . . .'

'It's a small affair but I think it may lead to bigger. In fact, something makes me sure it will do. And if it does I hope you'll not forget me.'

The nark eyed Edward. 'Oh, of course not,' Edward said.

'Briefly, then, I want you to meet a pimp.'

Edward looked interrogative and said nothing.

'Here's the whole tale. This pimp, unless I'm much mistaken, is offering something much more interesting than he seems to be.'

'Go on . . .'

'He works in a saloon bar not far from here: empty glass collector —you know—splendid opportunities for contacts. Well: when the pub closes lots of them, specially Irish, still want to go on drinking.'

'Naturally.'

'Naturally. So he leads them—some of them—to a Cyprus caff where they can get it after hours.'

'Not interested. Liquor cases? What you take me for?'

'*Do* be patient, officer' (last word uttered in an urgent whisper). 'In this speakeasy, I think they also gamble.'

'Still not interested.'

'*And* make other contacts.

'Which?'

'Girls.'

'That's better. On the premises?'

'No.'

'Then where?'

'I don't know.'

'Oh, *don't* you. Then how you know they go after girls if you don't know where they go to—that is, if you really *don't* know?'

The nark looked pained. 'You and I,' he said, 'are just not going to get anywhere unless we trust each other—up to a point, at any rate.'

'All right—I trust you: so?'

'That's all I ask. Now, listen. He takes them off from the Cyprus caff, this pimp, in *groups* and on *foot*—they don't take taxis. Also, they don't come back. Now, then: what else but girls would keep drunken men from going back again to a speakeasy that's a spieler?'

'If it's just single girls they go to, I'm still not interested.'

'I don't expect you would be. But *can* it be single girls? Off in a group ... no taxi ... he can't distribute them one by one around the area, can he?'

'So you think it's a brothel.'

The nark nodded sagely.

'That *might* interest me,' said Edward.

'I thought so.'

'But you: why haven't you followed them to make sure?'

The nark looked bland. 'Tell me—why should I? It might be dangerous, you know. And I don't want to be observed. Anyway, it's not what I'm paid to do. That's where I think possibly *you* come in.'

MR JUSTICE (STILL)

The Detective-sergeant had told Edward that 'if anything at all big comes up,' he was to inform him and not try to tackle it alone. 'If you prove to be any good,' his senior had added, 'something certainly *will* turn up, because a good copper always attracts crime to himself. But don't forget—it's only with arrest that the real problem of our job begins. There's the prisoner to be dealt with for his statement and so on, and beyond that the whole machinery of the courts we've got to persuade.' But Edward had vivid recollections of his disappointments when in uniformed days any discovery of his own produced, if reported, a host of seniors who did all the fancy work and took the credit. And knowing success is never blamed, he decided to chance his arm and handle the suspected brothel case alone.

Accordingly, and by appointment, he met the nark at the public-house in question: or rather the nark, as agreed, merely handed an empty glass at 10.15 pm (publican's time) to the individual he accused of being a pimp in order that Edward might be sure of his identity. That, so far as the nark was concerned, ended the proceedings: after this Edward was on his own.

The pimp, surprisingly, was little more than a teenager—twenty-one or two, Edward thought, and looking younger than his age. He was so surprised by the boy's appearance that against all professional etiquette he ventured a glance, in search of confirmation, at the nark—who very properly ignored it. The pimp, also, was a songster: for between his errands and still holding wallop-stained glasses in casual festoons, he'd pause at a microphone to nasally intone appalling Irish melodies much appreciated by the Celtic boozers who the farther they got from Erin's isle, adored it all the more.

At closing time, Edward lingered in the street carrying (a subtle touch, he thought) a quarter-filled can of paraffin whose purpose was that wherever he might be observed to loiter, the assumption would be he was visiting or coming from a neighbour to collect or supply this useful household fluid. At the back of his mind there was also the notion it might come in useful to hurl at somebody, if need be. For Edward was now learning what all young coppers do: that their job, at night, and even sometimes in the day can be very dangerous. The only security he felt was that he was alone: always the safest situation for any probing, nocturnal prowler. This wisdom confirmed the Detective-sergeant's diagnosis that he was born to the purple of the CID: who've soon understood the real reason why plain-clothes men are told to work, if possible, in pairs, is not for their own protection but that one can be the witness of an assault upon the other, and bring any vital messages home to base.

By now he was following a carolling party piloted by the pimp, the paraffin in his can playing lapping harmonies to their graceless melodies. The Cypriot café was not far off, and from its exterior Ted had no difficulty in observing they descended immediately to an invisible basement room. After a while of strolling and hesitation he entered, parked his paraffin tin, and ordered kebab and ladies' fingers. He ate these slowly and drank two Turkish coffees till he was the only surviving customer. Hints began to be dropped, even by the courteous Cypriots, that the time had come for him to be on his way. He therefore retreated to the road again, where he spent a tiresome, embarrassing hour of vigil.

But this delay served a purpose: his mounting irritation was now firmly concentrated on the drunks and gamblers in the cellar. Of course, he knew well—even recruit training had taught him that— you should always try to remain quite *impersonal* in your feelings about suspects, and not ever become too interested in them as individual human beings. On the other hand, a little spite and resentment would spice the eagerness to effect a capture. Edward was soon rewarded by the exaggeratedly cautious appearance of three Irishmen and the pimp. Observing (with recollections of the text-books) Alternative B, he 'followed' them from in front assisted, like a blind man's guide-dog (who, after all, doesn't know either *where* he's going), by the sound of their lurching feet behind. Soon the feet stopped, and he looked cautiously back to identify the brothel.

This word (brothel) conjured up scandalous, alluring visions. What it in London in most cases consists of is a dilapidated house with several girls in rooms with minimal accessories. But even in this basic, utilitarian form it still has, on account of the ancient mystique of the word and its frankly anti-social purpose (and the curiosity and venom these variously attract), a certain faded glamour. But not to Edward Justice. Edward did not condemn prostitutes because they were 'immoral': he did so because they sought to destroy in the most flagrant possible way his own deep belief in love. He therefore approached the establishment with intense interest and disapproval.

Lights shone from curtained windows, but the place was other- wise discreet. He knocked and nothing happened. Then he went away, returned and gave—a happy bow at a venture—three short knocks and one long. A light came on in the hall, the door opened hiding the person behind it, then closed on Edward who found him- self confronting a forty-ish man in jeans. 'I don't think we've met,' this person said.

'No. I'd like to see one of the girls.'

'Busy, mister. What you got in that can?'

'Oh, that? It's for the wife.'

'She know you're here?'

'Not likely.'

'No. Well, there it is. You can call back, or if you like you can have a Maxwell House with me downstairs while you're waiting for a vacancy.'

Edward accepted. The basement room was scented in a savagely 'oriental' manner, and its furnishings were the Harrow road emporium's version of Ali Baba's cave. The stranger put on a kettle, then surprised Edward considerably by trying to give him an affectionate kiss. He preserved his calm, however. 'You're one of those,' he said, disengaging politely.

'One of the many,' his host cried gaily. 'We horrid creatures crop up *every*where!'

'So you don't cause jealousies among the girls.'

'Oh, I wouldn't say *that*. After all, in a certain way they're very fond of me, and I'm very necessary to them, too.'

'You own this place, then?'

'*Me*? Living in the basement? Silly! No—I'm their maid.'

'A male maid, like.'

'Check!' cried the male maid, pouring water on the Maxwell House. 'And now,' he continued, bringing the coffee over, 'a question or two to *you*, please. Who sent you here?'

'The Cypriot boys.'

'Which one?'

'Dark feller.'

'Darling! *All* Cypriots are dark! Nicky, was it? Constantine?'

'Nicky, I think.'

The male maid shook his head at Edward. 'Naughty!' he said. 'There *is* no Nicky.'

'Well, mate, I don't know his bloody name but he just sent me.'

Hand on a jeaned hip, the male maid eyed him. 'Do you know what?' he said. 'I think I've been a very, very stupid boy. I think you're quite probably a c–o–p.'

'Who—me?'

'You, darling.'

The male maid, darting like a gold-fish, had raced through the door, slamming it behind him, and as Edward jumped up he heard the sound from the backyard behind of an outside lavatory chain being vigorously pulled up and down like a ship's siren. By the time he got to the first floor there were signs of considerable movement. Edward banged on the nearest door whence a loud female voice bellowed at him to fuck off. The second door on the landing opened, and he was face to face with a squat woman of thoroughly unwelcoming demeanour who, blocking the whole doorway, said to him, 'Let's see your warrant.'

'Open that door there,' said Edward.

'Listen, young man. Show me your warrant or else hop it. If you don't, I'm on the blower to Detective-constable you-know-who.'

'*Who?*'

'Who will *not* be pleased you've come here pissing in his garden.'

'What you mean?'

'Son, I'm beginning to think you're stupid. What you suppose I pay twenty a week for to you people? Get going, now. And sort it all out with your own mates: they'll tell you.'

By now doors had opened, figures appeared, and several very truculent males had gathered at strategic points on stairways. Silence fell a moment, and everybody watched. Edward had never felt so solitary in his life.

'You'll hear more of this,' he said, and walked downstairs. There were shouts of laughter and crude cries of abuse.

By the door, the male maid handed him his paraffin tin. Bursting with rage, Edward knocked it out of his hand, grabbed him and manhandled him out into the street. 'I'm being *arrested!*' cried the male maid. 'First time in *years*. A thrill!'

As he marched his capture up the dark and empty roads, Edward recalled as best he could in his emotion all the golden rules of an arrest: for this, though far from being his first, was his first one in the expert CID. He longed to get at his black note-book, for facts noted down in this, he knew, had a magical effect on juries and even magistrates. An officer, by law, can produce his notebook when in court and consult it (for matters of *fact* alone, of course) when in the witness-box. The conception that these factual jottings may be fantasies or added long after their supposedly immediate inscription—or that the defendant, too, might be permitted to produce a similar jury-impressing book—does not seem to have occurred to legislators. Edward knew all this: but to him the black book was the reassuring symbol of his office; and he liked to enhance the tenuous reality of the confusing happenings of fact by giving them, as soon as possible, this inscribed, oracular dimension.

But how do you get at your note-book if you're frog-marching a delightedly wriggling suspect in the dark? The more Edward thought of the whole episode the less he liked it. On a sudden decision he stopped at a corner, let the male maid go and said, 'All right—I'm turning you loose. Now skip!'

'Oh, *are* you!' said the maid, rubbing his skinny arms.

'Hop it now,' said Edward.

The male maid stood his ground and cried, 'Copper, I *refuse* to be released.'

Edward had not quite expected this. 'Oh?' he said, as nastily as possible.

'Look, big boy,' the atrocious male maid answered. 'You've messed things up for us tonight, and I'm going to mess up a thing or two for you.'

As to his next move, Edward didn't hesitate. He hit the male maid very hard in the face, and turned and walked away. When he paused after several hundred yards to make some notes of the occurrence (and of others) in his book, he was dismayed to see the maid still following at a distance. He hurried on; and reaching the highway, by the expedient of showing his card to a uniformed man and of declaring the male maid had urinated in a public place, he shook him off and returned (determined to say nothing of all this) to the station.

Immediately on arrival, he was sent for by the Detective-sergeant. This officer, more in exasperation than in anger, blew him up. 'You'd like to know,' he said to Edward, 'what you've done wrong. Well, I'll tell you: everything.'

'Sir?'

'First and foremost—and even *you* should know this, constable—you don't tackle *any* case—any case at all—without prior notification and permission unless, of course, it comes up on you suddenly like a smash-and-grab or something.'

'Yes, sir.'

'This is a *Force*,' the officer said. 'Not a collection of Robin Hoods.'

'No, sir.'

'Next. If you want to enter a house without a warrant, I've no objection: these little matters can usually be ironed out and brothels, of course, don't expect you to have one anyway. But *please* don't enter any house at all without first checking if your colleagues happen to know much more about it already than you ever will. Particularly, constable, any suspect premises we've decided to let stay open for our own particular purposes.'

'I'm sorry, sir, I don't . . .'

'I expect not. Look! That gaff, as gaffs up this way go, is perfectly well conducted and a very useful place indeed to pick up *real* suspects in: the sort of criminal you *should* be interested in.'

'I see, sir.'

'You see!'

'I suppose, sir,' Edward said cautiously, 'the woman phoned you . . . or someone.'

'Oh—brilliant! Let me tell you something, son. That good woman you upset is much more useful to the Force at present by her information than *you* look like shaping up to be.'

'Yes, sir.'

'And now you've crashed in there like a cow in a china-shop, what use is she going to be to us? Eh? Answer me that! Or *ask* me before you do these things. That's what I'm here for: come and ask me!'

'But sir,' said Edward full of contrition, 'brothels *are* often raided, aren't they? Brothel-keeping cases *do* come up . . .'

'Naturally, boy! But do use your loaf! You only raid the place when any advantages it may have to the Force are *less* than the prestige of a cast-iron brothel-keeping case. If vice has got to flourish, it had better flourish underneath our eyes until we're ready to clamp down on it.'

'Yes, sir.'

The Detective-sergeant lit his pipe. 'You'll soon see how it is,' he said. 'Sometimes, of course, the order comes to us from on high, and then we close the place up anyway. Or maybe the Madam forgets her place and fails to be co-operative. Or maybe there's a change of personnel here at the station and somebody new in charge just doesn't like her face. Those vice hustlers know all that, and so do we: the whole thing's perfectly well understood. Except, of course, by idiots like you.'

'Yes, sir.'

A constable entered, saluted and said, 'There's a poof downstairs, sir, wants to bring an assault charge.'

'Against who?'

The constable looked at Edward.

'Oh, no!' the Detective-sergeant cried. Then, to the constable, 'Throw him out.'

'He's very persistent, sir. He says if we won't wear it here he'll take it to another station.'

'*Does* he?' the Detective-sergeant said, an ominous glint appearing in his clouded eyes. 'Just wheel him in, constable, will you?' He then turned to Edward. 'You've broken,' he said, 'the first rule of the business: which is to make an arrest, and fail to bring a charge and make it stick.'

Edward said meekly, 'Can't we just charge him, sir, with being a queer?'

The Detective-sergeant didn't even bother to answer. The male maid appeared and the uniformed constable withdrew. The Detective-sergeant got up, punched the male maid five or six times very hard in an extremely dispassionate manner in the stomach, then threw him across a chair and said, 'I know you're a masochist and enjoy it, but don't provoke me or there might be an accident. Now, listen. What happened down at your place tonight just didn't happen. Do you understand? If I hear a squeak out of you, or anybody, I'm taking *you* in *not* on a vice charge which I know you wouldn't mind, but on a charge of robbing a client there and, believe me, everything will be present and correct: witnesses and stolen goods, your own sworn statement—the whole lot. You poofs have a high time in the nick, three in a cell, as we all well know. But this wouldn't be months I'd get you, sonny, it'd be years. And think of it, you might grow old and grey and unattractive, specially if I dropped a hint about you to the screws. So. Just apologize to my officer for all the trouble you've caused everyone, withdraw your charge as you pass the desk on your way out, and get back to bed again with your current husband.'

The male maid left in silence: though not without a yearning, reproachful glance at Edward.

Then the Detective-sergeant said: 'Now you, son. Please understand: I can't have anything more like this from you, either. You've got to improve your performance quite a bit or I'll lose my patience with you.'

'Yes, sir.'

'All right. Fuck off home.'

Edward stood at attention in salute, but hesitated before moving off. 'Well?' said the Detective-sergeant.

'Sir: it's just a question, sir, of procedure. This hitting them. I know the rule is you never do. But could you tell me please, sir, when you *can* do?'

A cracked smile appeared on the Detective-sergeant's life-battered countenance.

'Well, son,' he said, 'number one, in public, never. The citizens don't like it. Also, they don't believe we *do* it. Of course, if you're quite obviously attacked it's another matter.'

'Yes, sir. And in here?'

The Detective-sergeant rose and said, 'Well, constable, that depends. Personally, I don't happen to be a sadist and never do it unless it's clearly necessary to get certain results. Others do, I know, just for the heck of it: but not me.'

'No, sir.'

'If you *do* do it,' the officer continued, 'the first thing to remember is not to mark them: not to hit them where it shows next day in daylight. Never forget: they've got to be produced in court in twenty-four hours—or forty-eight, of course, if the day of arrest happens to be a Saturday.'

'And if you *do* happen to mark them, sir?'

'You say they went berserk and had to be restrained. Of course, you know—sometimes they do: I could show you a scar or two to prove it.'

'But, sir. If you bash them—don't they tell the magistrate?'

'Sometimes ... It has been known ... I've not met with one magistrate yet, though, who's believed it ... Or even if they do, well, so long as they think the charge you've made against the prisoner's quite authentic it doesn't seem to worry them unduly ... As for juries, if a prisoner pleads violence or a forced confession, in my experience all it does is tell against him in the verdict.'

'I see, sir.'

'Don't *rely* on that, though, constable. There's no point at all in using force just for the sake of it, unless it serves a purpose. Because —and you might as well remember this if you possibly can—your real battle isn't with the criminal but with the courts. It's only *there* that you can get him his conviction. You've got counsel up against you, and solicitors, and the witnesses for the defence, and juries and magistrates and judges—and the press, please don't forget *those* little parasites. They've all got to be defeated or convinced before your man gets his complimentary ticket for a seat in Brixton.'

'I'll remember, sir.'

'I do hope so. In the Force, constable, the greatest asset that a man can have, in my opinion, isn't all the ones you read so much about but purely and simply a sense of *order*: of thoroughly methodical procedure. If you train yourself to be methodical and avoid confusion like the plague, then you may end up Chief Constable—just think of that! Not, on your present showing, that it's very likely,' he added, turning out the light and opening the office door.

MR LOVE

A CHIEF difficulty in his new role, Frankie found, was what to do with the twenty-four hours of the day. At sea, this never had been a problem: even leisure, on board ship, seems to be purposeful: a relaxation from the tasks behind, a preparation for those ahead—time never seemed to *hang* upon a seaman's hands. Even to be unemployed was, in a sense, a full-time occupation: the hours it took to achieve the feat of the single minute's signing on at the Labour; the problems of where to sleep and how to eat, and even the sterile round in search of jobs.

But now his time-table except at certain immutable, vital points was vague in the extreme. He had to be home in his girl's new flat at Kilburn for the most important moment of their day—or night-and-day, for Frankie was finding the two radically divided sections were merging into one. This was the moment when, dismissing the last visitor, his girl produced the old black bag (to which in spite of growing prosperity she sentimentally clung) and shook its contents out upon the kitchen table. This was the hour of reckoning, the essential confrontation. Frankie must know *exactly* what she earned

—if she'd hid as much as a halfpenny their relationship would lose its fundamental basis. And she must know that *he* knew: what he then did with the money seemed of less importance to her, for she was quite un-grasping and, so long as she had what was necessary for essential housekeeping and personal adornment, she left the disposition of the funds entirely to him.

After this ceremony there was the continued proof, usually in the small hours, of Frankie's devotion to his girl. And then a number of minor but very important social imperatives: the Sunday evening visit, on her night off, to the Odeon; appearances at certain clubs which for professional purposes (but thoroughly indirect ones) she frequented; and occasional calls at lawyers' offices when minor difficulties arose, or were thought to be about to do so.

If Frankie had adhered to his original intention—backed by her own sage counsel—to get a cover job, a great many of these errands could no doubt have been avoided. But he had not. The reason wasn't simply that having enough money he didn't feel the need to: many rich men love work, after all. It was just that any sort of normal toil seemed quite incompatible with his position. In this he resembled the aristocrat who, appearing before the bankruptcy court, tells the judge with manifest and rather hopeless sincerity that he just couldn't find work appropriate to his status.

So there was a paradox (one of many now) in Frankie's life. On the one hand, time hung heavy on his hands and much ingenuity had to be expended in wasting it without total boredom. But on the other—this was the point—he *did* have the ever-present sensation of being *occupied*: of having if not a job, a function and even a 'function' in society. And apart from anything else, to remain constantly *available* so far as his girl was concerned, and constantly *watchful* himself in regard to the mysterious and ever-present law, did constitute a full-time activity of a kind.

As for the disposal of the money, this had its problems too. A growing acquaintance with his fellow ponces (which Frankie had tried to avoid but which, just as with fellow mariners on board ship, was really quite inevitable) had shown him that by and large they fell (as with all other human creatures) into two sharply divided categories: the spenders and the savers. The chief stratagem by which spender-ponces relieved themselves of the intolerable burden of holding on to money they had coveted so eagerly, was by gambling: but Frankie had tried this and found it unbearably meaningless and dull—even if he won as, being indifferent, he often did. Others invested in huge wardrobes or fast cars: but this, except among the pin-headed, was considered most unwise for it was a gross and needless provocation of the law. It was true, of course, that a great many of the more foolish girls loved their men to spend the money in this way, as a taste for visible riches bound the man to them all the closer; and its fruits were the manifest proof of their own success in their business.

As for the savers, whose usual intention was to 'cut out' one day with the girl (or possibly without her) to start a business of some kind, the chief disadvantage was that they were usually grudging and unattractive characters (as Frankie Love was not) and more, that to be a business *man*, even if a ponce, you need a business *head*: which Frankie knew he hadn't got at all. And his determination to save had been baulked, as the girl had foreseen, by the acute danger of opening any sort of an account and by his genuine reluctance to have all the money in her name: for the whole meaning of the symbolic emptying of the bag at night—the gesture which bound him absolutely to her—would have been lost if the money went back from the bag into an account that she controlled.

He therefore hit on an expedient that would have seemed inconceivable a few months ago. Frankie, like most proletarian Europeans, despised Asiatics to such a degree that you could hardly even call it contempt (quite unaware, like millions of his countrymen, that this feeling was reciprocated by Asians at much profounder levels). But in his predicament it suddenly occurred to him that throughout his considerable commerce with them, no Asian had ever robbed him: exasperated him, yes, but never deceived him over money. He accordingly approached, with the girl's full approval, her former Stepney landlord, the Bengali, and suggested that the Bengali should hold his money for him (*not* for her) on the understanding no interest whatever need be paid. With splendid visions of the acquisition of additional slum property which he could let out for vice, or for honest purposes to his fellow-countrymen at exorbitant rentals in a country that denies accommodation to a man of colour, the Bengali immediately agreed.

A man of some intelligence cannot fail, in any environment where fate thrusts him, to become interested in its workings however much he may dislike or disapprove of them. Thus reluctant, scholarly conscripts study regimental histories, and professional men who've fallen by the wayside write excellent studies about jails. In much the same spirit Frankie, despite himself, became interested in whores and ponces. And though not easily given to casual friendships he already had several acquaintances among the men—the women, so far as possible, he kept politely at a distance not because he was afraid of them in any way, but because this was the very basis of his bargain with his girl.

Among these pals there was a star ponce whom Frankie had got to know at a drinking-club patronized by the men of his profession. As with actresses or television personalities in the outer world, there is, in that of prostitution, a fashion at any particular moment for this or that ponce or whore: the less stable of the girls all endeavouring to hook the star ponce, and the less satisfied of the ponces trying to transfer their allegiance to the star whore of the moment. Dreadful quarrels, often accompanied by violence and sensational denunciations, accompany these struggles: but above all of them this star ponce friend of Frankie's rode serene. He *knew* he was a star—did not his glittering attire and his relaxed and glowing mien testify eloquently to the fact? But he was genuinely devoted to his girl and was—not unusual, perhaps surprisingly, among ponces— exceedingly good-natured. So he parried the manoeuvres of the eager whores with deft evasions and even managed not to arouse the jealousies of the men. 'It's a world!' he would say to Frankie (or Francis, as for some reason he always called him) when they sat to- gether at the drinking-club in masculine communion.

The star ponce was Cornish and had been at sea, and shared with Frankie a deep disdain for all the multitudes who haven't. 'The sea,' he told Frankie, 'teaches you the scale of things: what matters and what really doesn't. The only ceremony I've ever seen that im- pressed me in the least is a sea burial: no priest, only the captain; no mourners, only the mates; no earth and worms or fire and ash-cans, but the huge sea and the fishes sailing gently through your eyes.'

'Or a ship's court,' said Frankie. 'Ever seen one of those? The old man a judge who really *knows*; and witnesses who nobody's been getting at; and sailors for your jury who know all about you and your case first hand.'

'Why did we leave it, Francis?'

'Ask yourself that, quartermaster,' Frankie said.

The star ponce beckoned for refills. When the girl (who'd brought the glasses voluntarily, for there was no service in the club) had been thanked and gone, he said to Frankie, 'That one's got her eye on you.'

'Yes, I noticed.'

'Not interested, Francis?'

'One at a time.'

'How right you are!' The star ponce smiled. 'Mind you, you can stick to one and still have others.'

'You can?'

'Some manage it. Even three or four at a time.'

'Sharp operators! And the girls know?'

'Usually the wires get crossed—and then they do. Not easy, as you can imagine, flitting from one address to another without running out of excuses and vital energy.'

'Those boys deserve their money. And the girls wear it?'

'Naturally, there are rows—a thing I personally hate. But sometimes if they're fond of the boy, even if they *do* know they accept it.'

'Who understands women?'

'Only they do.'

The star ponce offered panatellas. 'Ever thought of getting wed?' he said.

'To *her*?'

'Yeah.'

'Why should I?'

'Well—there could be reasons.'

'Such as what?'

'You might like to: like her, I mean.'

'That's a good one . . . Any others?'

'She might like it, too. And it makes them long-suffering, Francis, if you're a husband.'

'Not so likely to speak out of turn, you mean?'

'Not *quite* so likely: and she can't appear in court against you as your wife, though she can still chat about you to the coppers.'

'But does it impress the courts at all—your being married?'

'Oh, not in the least. The nicks are full of married ponces. No: it's just rather nice, that's all.'

'You done it?'

'No . . .'

'I see.'

They puffed away like two young rising statesmen. 'Getting used to the life?' the star ponce asked.

'Except for a few particulars.'

'Yeah?'

'Still can't get used to all that *money*.'

'Nor me: after all these years.'

'Really! When you think of the *millions* the mugs spend! We must be a race of randy, frustrated fools.'

'Speak for yourself: I'm Cornish. Anything else?'

'Yes. When people ask me what I *do*. I can't quite get used to that.'

'You say seaman?'

'Yes. But I know *I* don't believe it any longer.'

'I say turf accountant. I've found it explains my movements best.'

'Don't they try to place bets?'

'Sometimes . . . The question was awkward in the nick as well.'

'You been in there?'

'Didn't I tell you? One three, one six: next time's dangerous.'

'Let's hope there'll be none. And what did you tell them all in there?'

The star ponce looked ruminative and grave. 'Poncing and rape of minors are the two things criminals won't wear. Even poofs they will, but not we two. They're great snobs, the real professionals, about what a man's in for.'

'So what did you tell them?'

'That was it. I thought: well, I *am* a ponce—so what? I said poncing.'

'And?'

'They crunched me.'

'Nice! What did you say the next time?'

'Fraudulent conversion. That was quite all right. They were quite respectful.'

Frankie drank. 'They're hard on us, aren't they, in this world,' he said.

The star ponce said, 'Very. And yet—there are those two things. If there weren't any clients there couldn't be any ponces, let alone any whores. Have they thought of that at all?'

'I don't suppose so.'

'If no one will buy a product, no one will sell it or profit by its sale.'

'Just so.'

'And as for where the blame lies, if there is any, well, for every one of us and each one of our girls there must be several hundred clients or more.'

'It's mathematical.'

The star ponce turned his glorious eyes on Frankie. 'I'll tell you a thing,' he said. 'It's a triangle that won't stand up without any one of its three sides: client and whore and ponce. If the clients don't like us, well, it's simple: they should just stop being clients.'

'Then the triangle collapses.'

'But it won't! That's just the point, it won't, and everyone knows it. That's why all these new laws just shift the problem without altering it in any way at all. Because the girl, and her friend, and the man dropping in from somewhere, are as old as the Garden of Eden and even older.'

'There were only two of them in there,' said Frankie.

'Well, Adam must have doubled.' The star ponce stiffened slightly. 'Don't look now. But when you do you'll see we've got two coppers on the premises: one he, one she. Behind the telly set.'

'They come here often?' Frankie said, not looking up.

'Weekly or so—routine. Why they bother to dress up like that I can't imagine, but they prefer it that way.'

Frankie observed the couple. They looked like a pair of elderly teenagers: the man in Italian drape and pointeds with a Tab Hunter hair-do, the woman with puff-pastry locks, flowered separates, paper nylon petticoat and white stilettos. They were engaged in animated conversation intended to disguise the fact that no one else wished to speak to them: though no one, of course, would have refused to do so if invited.

'Poor fuckers,' said the star ponce. 'What must it feel like, earning your living spying on your fellow men?'

'How do they pay for all that clobber?' Frankie asked. 'Do they get expenses?'

'Not on that scale. Talk to the club owner here: he'll tell you.'

'Something for protection?'

'District-nurse money, he calls it. For their healing visits. Still, I prefer those fancy vice boys to the poker-faced lot in uniform. They may be crooked, but in my experience a man who's crooked is in some way or other human. Almost, anyway.'

Frankie looked at the star ponce and said, 'You afraid of them?'

'Who—me?' The star ponce reflected. 'Well—yes, of course,' he said, 'but not of *them*: I mean, I'm not scared of them individually or even several. I've been alone in the cells with them, Francis, and no holds barred, and I've found I haven't been afraid. But of the Force—yes, I am. You see, we come and go—and even they do: but the Force—it goes on forever.'

'Just like the world does.'

'Yes, on forever. There's always this, you see. If they really decide to turn the heat on anyone—not just one of us, but I mean on *any*one—well, they can always find *something*, can't they.'

'Or say they do . . . which amounts to much the same.'

The star ponce shook his luscious locks and said, 'Well, not exactly. If ever they get *you* in the cells, Francis, remember this. The trial's not there, it's in the open court. The mistake almost everyone makes, even quite clever people and no doubt because they're scared, is to fall for the copper's spiel of pretending it's *he* who conducts the trial. Well—it's not: there's always the lawyers and the judges.'

'So I'm discovering.'

'Well—remember it. Anyone can come unstuck, but you lessen the chances quite a bit if you remember . . . *never* speak to them. If six men try to carve you up—don't call a copper: grin and bear it. Then, if they knock you off, don't *talk*: Francis, don't ever talk. Name, address and age, that's all: just like the navy or the army. And never plead guilty—never. Because to them, whoever you are, if they take you you *are* guilty, so it makes no difference anyway. If they find you outside the Bank of England with a bag of gold—not guilty. In the courts, there's always a chance: if you talk to them or commit yourself to any plea, there's none.'

'I'll remember,' said Frankie, finishing his glass.

The star ponce emptied his too and rose. 'All the same,' he said, 'in this business, however careful you may be, you've *always* got to listen for the knock on the front door. Whenever you hear a knock, even if it's only the Plymouth Brethren calling to save souls, you've got to be alert and ready. And take your time before you open up: if they *really* want to see you, don't be in a hurry: they can always break the door down—and they will.'

MR JUSTICE

EDWARD longed to escape from the thraldom of the section-house. When he did his military service he didn't really dislike barrack-rooms—realized, in fact, that if you had to be a soldier they were the most practical and even comfortable places to be a soldier in. But in the section-house the men were all rather older, and, except for a few widowers and what is known as 'hardened' bachelors, all anxious, like him, not to be there any longer, since it wasn't really necessary for coppers to live in great male dormitories. Besides, the atmosphere of *randiness* in the place—you could only call it that—depressed him: you could feel it bursting from the rooms at night, and in the mess-hall the conversation (when it wasn't gossip about the Force) centred on 'sex' monotonously. For Edward, sex was a secret and yet a totally splendid thing: something he felt no need (like some copper puritans) to be uncomfortable about at all—very much the contrary—but one that lost all its glory and delight once it was severed, even in conversation, from the loved person who ex-changed it with you.

But how to leave the section-house? The Force didn't care much for single men in lodgings; and marriage to his girl was for the moment, anyway, impossible. His sexual trysts with her at present took place at her father's house with his reluctant connivance (a reluctance, in respect of these particular premises, that Edward fully shared), or sometimes dangerously at the houses of several friends (for the trouble with friends is that they can betray you by their quite benevolent intentions), and even, on one or two ex-

tremely chancy occasions, in public places: a thing Edward had
professionally a horror of, since so many who used the outer woods
and gardens did so for reasons that were utterly perverse. It seemed
to him that the only (relatively) safe procedure would be for her to
take rooms at some discreet address, and for him to visit her there
with maximum discretion likewise.

This plan he unfolded in the small back garden of her father's
house in Kensal Green, while the older man morosely eyed them
through the back window of the kitchen where he was engaged on
his part-time trade of mending radio and telly sets and cameras and
high-grade gadgets—a free-lance occupation Edward did not approve of since it had something imprecisely *shady* about it. (Somehow all those sets looked stolen, not left for repair, and anyway,
how did the older man make all those contacts to get the jobs? And
wasn't this still, in spite of all his promises, a cover story?) The back
garden—yard, really—was hemmed in by walls and windows, but
his girl and he were in its most secluded corner, and Edward
(though even naked he'd have looked just as much a copper) had on
very casual, un-professional attire. The girl poured tea and *listened*
to him in that attentive, respectful way that women have when they
hear of some plan to which they may or may not agree, but know it
to be dear to their lover's heart and in its intentions, anyway, con-
ducive to their own interests and a proof of his attachment.

'The chief obstacles,' Edward said, 'are these. Money first. Well—
that's not really a problem with our joint earnings, and you know
I'm not a spender; also—you never know—I may get some extra—
expenses or something—to help out. Premises. That really shouldn't
be difficult if we look carefully *and*—here's the important point—
are willing to pay enough: say even five or six a week. Then . . . well,
the whole set-up. If we take care I don't think we should attract
attention, particularly if we get a place in a block that's big enough:
I mean like some council flats, say, with stacks of tenants in them.
Of course, everyone who's interested will know perfectly well why I
visit you, but that doesn't really matter unless there's any trouble-
makers among them who start shooting off their mouths. Naturally,
I'll have to check carefully to see if there happen to be any other
coppers living in the block. If not, then well and good, let's go
ahead. And remember: we won't actually be doing anything *illegal*,

will we. The worst I can expect, if the Force should discover, is a good ticking-off—and also, perhaps, some enquiries about you which may very well lead home to your Dad. (Edward glanced at the window and caught his potential father-in-law's baleful eye.) But that we'll have to leave to chance—we can't foresee *every*thing, can we. The chief question that then remains is—when can I visit you? I'll have to check in at the section-house to sleep fairly often, and you've got your job to go out to during the day. So that leaves us week-ends, and also the evenings when I can plead duty or actually be out on it and spare a moment. They don't check on our time much, see, in the present job: they trust us to get on with it, and all they ask for is results.'

'I think I might know a place,' the girl said.

'Yeah? What area? Obviously, it can't be too far—unless I could get hold of a motor-bike, which might in a way be better.'

'In Kilburn,' she said.

'Up there? Well, it's a nice, quiet . . . well, *neutral* sort of area, isn't it. What particular place had you got in mind?'

'A girl at the workshops lives with her husband and kids there. And she told me you can jump the queue if you give something to the janitor. It's working-class, you know, but a privately owned block, not the municipal. So the rents are a bit high, too.'

'All this is going to need money,' Edward said. 'And that reminds me. Darling, whatever you do, *don't* take any from your father.'

'No, I know about that.'

'He's in the clear now, of course, but if you had even a penny from him, and a bit of it went to me even in a round-about way, it just wouldn't do.'

'No.'

Edward finished his fourth tea. 'And another thing,' he said. 'As soon as you're in, you'd better get on the phone.'

'I'd thought of that,' she said.

'A lot of our meetings will have to be at short notice, and that's the best way we can fix them discreetly without wasting time.'

The girl got up. 'All right,' she said. 'If you've got the time to spare now, Ted, we might take a walk over and have a look at the place.'

They went in through the back basement entrance and up the

inside stairs. The girl opened the kitchen door to say a word to her father, but when Edward tried to say goodbye to him he turned up a radio to a horrid blare. 'I really don't know why your Dad dislikes me so much,' Edward said to her as they walked across towards Queen's park. 'I know he's a copper-hater, but why should he detest me personally?'

'On account of his past,' said the girl, taking his hand and intimately locking up his fingers. 'He was framed, so he says, as you know, and you really must make allowances.'

'Oh, they all say that.'

'Yes, Ted: but it does happen, doesn't it.'

Edward sighed. The subject had come up before in his life, and by now he'd grown to live with it and it bored him. 'Well, it does,' he said. 'But in ninety-nine cases out of a hundred, even more I'd say, a case is never fixed unless we're absolutely sure the feller did it.'

'If you're all that sure, why can't you prove it properly?'

'Because that's often very, very difficult: you'd be surprised. There's laws of evidence, and legal quibbles if the case is defended, and sometimes even the old judge, though he may know as well as we do that the prisoner's guilty, brings up some act of Queen Victoria's reign or maybe earlier that destroys our case.'

The girl reflected. 'But if you fix a case, Edward, then don't you commit a crime yourself?'

'What crime? Oh, you mean perjury.'

'It *is* a crime, isn't it?'

'Oh, of course! But not, as I see it, for us officers. In the first place let me tell you, if we didn't use it there'd be stacks of known and previously convicted criminals who we'd never manage to put away at all. And then, there's another thing. You must remember, dear, that we're the only people who have to appear constantly in the courts in dozens of cases under oath. Now, if it's just the single defendant coming up once or twice—or even, let's say, as many as fifty times in his life—he only has to face the perjury problem—if it *is* one to him—on those individual occasions. But us, we have to face it every week almost of our lives. Could we *ever* be all that scrupulous? Then, there's this. Even suppose the case is straight and all our evidence is kosher. Suddenly, out of the blue, from the counsel who's cross-examining or even from our own feller for the Crown, you may get a question—one that's really got little or nothing to do with the case at all—which you simply cannot answer factually without prejudicing the whole issue. And then most of all, dear, there's your superior officers you've got to consider. Suppose Detective-inspector So-and-so says "Constable, this is the way we're handling this case"—what do I do? Tell him he's got it wrong?'

'Yes, I see all that,' she answered. 'But doesn't it mean if you commit perjury yourself that the defendant's bound to do it too, whether he wants to or not?'

'I don't see that—how come?'

'According to Dad, when the case was cooked up against him . . .'

'Cooked up!'

'Well, arranged . . . his solicitor advised him that if he denied everything the witnesses for the Force said, no one on earth—and certainly no one on the jury—would ever believe him. So he played along with their story part of the way, and just denied certain essentials. But even that didn't help him in the end . . .'

'Well, there it is, dear: that's how it goes.'

'And what's more, he says the fact you mentioned just now, Ted, that your officers have such a long experience of giving evidence makes any prisoner like an untrained amateur up against professionals.'

'Well—that's what we are. And really, dearest, the whole question about your old Dad is—did he do it or didn't he? That's what you've really got to decide before you pass any judgment on all of us.'

They were now out of Queen's park. He thought and said (a note of indignation in his voice), 'You know *really*, the public expect just a bit too much from us, don't they? They all want convictions and howl if we don't succeed in getting them! And all the responsibility for winning the cases by the right presentation of the evidence —which *has* a certain risk involved, even to us, let alone any question of our own feelings in the matter—well, *all* that responsibility *we* take off the public's shoulders on to our own. And then people turn round and tell us we *fix* all these cases.'

His fingers were clutching hers. She took a more gentle grip and said, 'Don't be upset, Ted: I *do* understand. And I dare say the judges and magistrates do as well.'

'But of course!' he cried. 'Some of them are quite simple in spite of all their law books, and don't really understand, maybe. But most of them realize that crime's *got* to be suppressed and provided we don't slip up over the technicalities they never enquire too closely into our actual methods. And that goes for all the top people in the business—I'm not speaking of the thousands of mugs, even the educated quite influential ones—but the people who really *know* the law and how it operates. They know what we do, and they know why we do it and they accept it. They never say so, of course. And if we slip up, they're pitiless. But they know.'

Near by Paddington cemetery she stopped beside the stones and railings and reached up and kissed him, without reservation of her person, warmly, entirely—a whole gift. He was soothed and enchanted because at such moments she gave him to himself: for not even the Force could offer him such self-realization as she did when she brought her love to him so utterly that he was unaware of her—only of himself. 'If only we could marry now,' he whispered into her hair. She held him closer, yet not *tight* as some girls do. A professional instinct made him cut short the embrace, though gently, and they entered together the respectable wastes of Kilburn.

Examining the area, Edward liked it. There is about Kilburn a sort of faded respectability, of self-righteous drabness, that appealed to him. For the true copper's dominant characteristic, if the truth be known, is neither those daring nor vicious qualities that are sometimes attributed to him by friend or enemy, but an ingrained conservatism, an almost desperate love of the conventional. It is untidiness, disorder, the unusual, that a copper disapproves of most of all: far more, even, than of crime, which is merely a professional matter. Hence his profound dislike of people loitering in streets, dressing extravagantly, speaking with exotic accents, being strange, weak, eccentric or simply any rare minority—of their doing, in short, anything that cannot be safely predicted.

So Kilburn was reassuring: but on the other hand it had something else that equally appealed to Edward which was that, although proper, it was also in an indefinable way equivocal. As you walked through its same and peeling (though un-slummy) streets, the façades of the houses hinted, somehow, that all was not as it seemed behind those faded doors and walls. This straitlaced seediness, this primped-up exterior behind which lurks something dubious and occasionally horrifying, is the chief feature of whole chunks of mid-twentieth-century London—as, indeed, of many of its inhabitants: the particular English mixture of lunacy and violence flourishing inside persons, and a décor, of impeccable lower-middle-class sedateness. This atmosphere appealed to Edward who, like all coppers, shunned clear pools (and even turbulent torrents) and preferred those whose surface, though quite still, could easily be stirred up into muddy little whirlpools. For if the copper is a worshipper of the conventional (so far as the world at large outside him is concerned), he is also in his inner person (being the arch empiricist) something of an anarch: a lover of stress and strain and conflict, wherein he himself may operate behind that outward, visible order he admires.

The flats the girl had in mind were of more recent construction—one of those countless anonymous 1950 blocks which, in spite of their proliferation, have as yet entirely failed to transform London from what it still after years of bombing and re-building essentially remains—a late-Victorian city. The block was tall and oblong-square and bleak and domestically adequate: perfect, in fact, for their intentions.

'Okay dear,' said Edward. 'You check with your friend and find out what the score is on the financial side, and I'll consult files and sources—very discreetly, of course—to find if anything's known to us about it. If both things tally, well, let's move in. I'm really getting tired, when I see you, of having to act as if I was a criminal.'

'The key money may be quite a bit,' she said. 'Something like fifty, I should imagine.'

Edward winced. 'Well, that's not the chief difficulty,' he said. 'Our chief obstacle is the place: if we find that's all right, the money will look after itself—it'll have to.'

He pressed her two arms, but only so, because the place was too public now for kissing; and each of them felt as well that the unknown tenants of the block were already curious neighbours. He ran for a bus and sat in a rear seat, eyeing his fellow travellers with the proprietory air of his profession as if they were all (and, indeed, the entire population of our islands) the potential inhabitants of some vast, imaginary jail. Passing the Metropolitan theatre of varieties he glanced out idly, and immediately left the bus. For he had noticed a person there whom an inborn and constantly developing instinct told him he should watch and follow.

This person set off along the Harrow road in the direction of the monumental metal bridges over the tangle of lines just outside Paddington railway station. The person's glances at certain passing citizens, all of a particular nature, confirmed Edward's suspicions of his hopes. At a square green metal urinal stuck on to a tall wall like a carbuncle, the person paused, gazed around (Edward was standing blandly at a bus stop), and entered. Five minutes elapsed: too long for nature and for innocence, and Edward pounced.

The design of male urinals, in England, and especially those dating from the heroic period of pre-World War I construction, has to be witnessed to be believed. For this simplest of acts, what one can only describe as temples, or shrines, have been erected. The larva-hued earthenware, the huge brass pipes, the great slate walls dividing the compartments, are all built on an Egyptian scale. Each visitor is isolated from his neighbour, though so close to him and in such physical communion, as if in a sort of lay confessional. Horrorpendous notices advising not to spit in the only place in the city where it wouldn't matter in the slightest, and warnings against fell diseases that can nowadays be cured by a few cordial jabs by a nurse in either buttock, abound, as do those reminding visitors about what their mothers taught them when, at the age of three or so, they were put into their first short pants. All this seems to bear witness to a really sensational and alarming fear and hatred of the flesh, even in its most natural functions, that inspired the municipal Pharaohs who designed these places. And from their ludicrous solemnity, and ribald inscriptions on the walls of a political, erotic, or merely autobiographical nature are an agreeable light relief.

As Edward expected, the person he had followed was up to no good at all and taking his place casually and, as it were, sympathetically in the adjacent compartment, he waited for his victim to make a fatal gesture. This, sure enough, he did. Whereupon Edward, making sure they were alone together, stepped quickly back behind the evildoer, said, 'I'm an officer of the law: I want to speak to you outside,' and hustled his prisoner out, barely giving him time to obey the injunction of an infantile nature just described.

Edward hurried his case along with a firm and dexterous grip, yet one which to a casual observer might seem that of a companion—perhaps a bit over-demonstrative, but certainly not ill-disposed. Round a corner, and over the western railway, they reached a lofty and secluded street.

Edward had said nothing yet (nor had the prisoner) and was, in fact, not quite sure what he was going to say. A charge of this kind, at the station, was always the subject of facetious comment, and on the part of a young CID man would certainly be esteemed detrimental to his prestige. In addition, as Edward well knew, there was the complication that it is very difficult to make such charges stick if the officer arrests the prisoner alone. In such a case, if the prisoner denies with resolution, it is one man's word against another's; and though the courts will probably believe the copper's, they prefer corroborative evidence and are apt to dismiss the case if they don't get it. The whole exploit was, in fact, an optimistic stab in a considerable darkness, and Edward had already decided to turn the prisoner loose after one of those lecturettes so gratifying to a young officer's ego. But at this moment the prisoner uttered plaintively the magic words, 'Officer, can't we talk this thing over?'

Any experienced copper knows instantly what this means. For unless the prisoner is an imbecile—that *does* happen, of course—he will know perfectly well there's no point whatever in talking anything over once the arrest is made, unless . . .

Edward stopped, backed the prisoner against a mews wall, still holding him firmly and discreetly, and said to him, 'Well?'

'I'm in your hands,' the prisoner said, 'and I don't want this thing to go any further. I'm a married man.'

'So?' Edward said.

There was a slight pause as they eyed each other well beyond the eyes. 'I've got a fiver in my pocket if you'll let me get at it,' the prisoner said.

'Have you?' said Edward, gazing at his victim with implacable denial. 'You know what an offer of that nature means?'

'I've got six or seven in all,' the prisoner said. 'That's all I've got: honest: you can search me.'

'Who are you?' said Edward.

'I'd rather not say my name.'

'Wouldn't you! Tell me what's your job.'

'Salesman.'

'Of what?'

'Vacuum cleaners.'

'With a suit like that? And that wrist watch?' Edward gave the man a wrench.

'All right. Car salesman. And I'll make it twenty.'

Edward, still holding him, put his face closer and said low, slow, and distinctly, 'You'll make it fifty. And you'll tell me where you work, and at exactly this time tomorrow—*exactly*, you understand me?—I'll be calling there *with* a colleague. And you, you'll have made arrangements to meet us alone in some room there—I don't care *where*—and hand me what I said, singles and not new ones *and* un-marked please, in a plain envelope, and then I'll forget about the whole matter and so will you. If you've got any ideas of seeing a lawyer or having any sort of reception committee for me, that's up to you. But don't forget my story will be—and it'll be ready for filing by tonight at the station—that I was unable to arrest you because on more important duties, but you attempted to commit an offence and attempted bribery to an officer in the due course of his duties. Is that quite clear?'

'I haven't got that money,' the prisoner said.

'Then you'll *get* it.'

'Fifty's a lot,' he cried.

'Quietly! So's a few weeks in the nick. You're certainly not a first offender . . .'

'I've never had a conviction . . .'

'We'll soon put that right for you if you don't do as I say. And one last thing. If you try to cross me over this you may get away with it, and you may not, but believe me, son, whatever embarrassment it might cause me, a lot of my colleagues in the Force won't like it at all, and once we've got the needle into a man that's shopped an officer, particularly a man like you, we'll see it goes in deep and *hurts* you.'

Edward gave the man a sharp twist and abruptly released him. 'Very well, officer,' he said. 'It'll be as you say.'

Edward looked at him, said nothing for a moment, and then after collecting some particulars briskly (as if at the prisoner's request), turned and walked away. Like a young soldier in battle who shoots and is shot at the first time, he felt pure elation: far greater than that in distant earlier days, of his first uniformed arrest. Then, as professional prudence descended on him again, he meditated on all the angles he could see so far. The rendezvous at the man's own office seemed to him the master-stroke. For what officer, suspected of corruption, would ever go to fetch a bribe in so compromising a place? Righteous indignation could greet any such suggestion! The only tricky moment would be leaving the office with the envelope. But he wouldn't: he'd bring the man out *with* the envelope, and take it from him somewhere else.

There only remained, so far as he could see, one problem: where to keep the money once he had it. Obviously, it would be imprudent to put even a relatively small lump sum like this in the Post Office savings—his only bankers. And perhaps as time passed, the sums might well get larger. And so? He must try to find out what the precedents in this matter in the Force might be, and even possibly consult his girl about it also.

MR LOVE

FRANKIE and his woman were well settled in: and hitherto, so far as they could see, had attracted no undue attention. Key money had been duly paid to the janitor of the block of flats they'd chosen —but since this was normal practice, excited no untoward remark. Frankie, though he still had no job, departed at fairly regular intervals as if to work, and was careful to remain quite soberly dressed—as much, so it happened, by inclination as by prudence. His girl put it about (but very casually, and without overdoing it at all) that her man had had an accident at sea and had retired, though so young, from active duty. Everyone knew, of course, that they weren't married; but this state of affairs was far from unusual among the tenants as a whole. As for the very essential maid to assist the girl in her profession, they'd decided to do without one both for caution's sake and for the following reason.

It was clearly necessary to have, if *asked* (no need to volunteer the information otherwise), an explanation of the visitors to Frankie's flat. Of course, in the girl's new status in her calling, the prices had gone up from those of Stepney days, so that fewer clients paid a greater total; but still some reason might be needed, not, perhaps, that there were so many visitors, but that so many of them—almost all, in fact—were men. In this dilemma, Frankie's woman had recourse to her old Mum: who being part gypsy, practised as faith-healer, in which art, over the years, she'd built up a considerable clientele especially among what one might call the contemporary *levellers*: small, nonconformist tradespeople who scorned received religions, scorned hospitals (except when, as sometimes happened, they were carried in there to die), scorned dignity and the intellect —scorned everything except the dogmatic certitude of their own infallibility.

The faith-healing Mum was reluctant to shift her practice entirely from Walthamstow, where she was a figure of some local weight, to Kilburn; nor did Frankie, who didn't care much for the old lady, wish to have her living in the flat. Accordingly she came across, often transported by a gratefully healed patient with a car-hire business, on certain evenings and afternoons; and to those who were at all curious about Frankie's woman the hint was dropped that the mother was initiating her daughter into the mysteries of her healing art.

The Mum, whose own legal record was unblemished, knew all she needed to about her girl's activities and accepted them entirely without censure. In her eyes, her daughter had not 'gone wrong' but merely gone slightly bent. Her attitude, perhaps, resembled that of an Inland Revenue collector whose daughter, unpredictably, has chosen to become an air-hostess: a tricky, odd profession, but one of evident advantage and repute. To Frankie she was far from cordial. She quite accepted the need for his existence, just as the hypothetical collector would have done the need of his daughter to be associated, professionally, with a pilot. It was just that she didn't *like* him: thought him a bit superior, ungrateful and, possible worse, untrustworthy.

The girl had furnished the flat in decorous and thoroughly petty-bourgeois style: it startlingly resembled those of countless other tenants of the building with its furnishings which, though solid, rather overstated their real degree of luxury. As the flat was quite

exiguous, Frankie had caused some inconvenience by absolutely refusing to allow the bed he shared with her, to be shared by anyone
else. Another, disguised as a 'divan', was therefore imported into the
living-room, taking up too much space and forcing the Mum (and
indeed Frankie, on the rare occasions he was present during business hours) to move into the kitchen, or his own bedroom. But as no
arrangement, whatever, here below, is ever precisely as each one of
the parties involved would wish it, the various give-and-takes were
generally accepted. What anyone else, including the janitor, thought
of the set-up—if they did think of it at all—remained unknown. But
in prostitution, as in all other businesses, if reasonable precautions
are taken any troubles are best not nervously foreseen, but reso-
lutely faced if they should arise.

The routine of a call-girl had, for Frankie, one very big surprise.
The life of a street whore in Stepney, from the little he'd seen of it,
was certainly not lacking in incident and colour; and for street-girls
in general, he supposed, excitement of some kind or other had been
the order of every day. But for a girl 'on the phone' the life was
colourless and business-like in the extreme. Those who telephoned,
and who were never accepted unless already known or strongly
recommended and never, even then, if proposing to bring strangers
or manifestly drunk, arrived discreetly and departed likewise: even
more anxious, it seemed, than Frankie's girl was, not to get involved
in 'anything'.

There were as was inevitable occasional 'incidents', at none of
which, hitherto, Frankie had himself been present—except once or
twice off-stage in the capacity of number-one reserve; but on such
occasions the trouble-maker had to face the formidable duo of
Frankie's woman and her Mum or even—still formidable enough
—Frankie's girl, operating solo. For she had the gift, common to
most women and even the un-respectable, of making any man who
steps out of line from the particular convention that he shares for
the moment with her appear, even to himself, to be crudely and
abysmally *wrong*.

Occasionally when Frankie timed things badly, rather dreary little
tea-parties took place between himself, his girl, and her appalling
Mum: on which occasions he was much vexed by their custom of
ignoring him almost, or of treating him at best as a visitor in his

own home or as a sort of bright young cousin: indispensable in his way, as all men must be admitted to be, but superfluous to so many of the vital feminine preoccupations. These trios would sometimes lead to rows and even, when Frankie and his girl were left alone, to violence: but it was difficult to quarrel with them, because they greeted his resentment with such totally unfeigned surprise. What on earth was eating up the boy? Goodness! he must be right out of his foolish mind!

'If an agent takes the money from the *girl*,' Frankie's woman was explaining in a conversation with her mother about the legal technicalities of brothel-keeping, 'that's an offence, yes, but not if he takes it from the *man*.'

They both glanced at Frankie.

'As things are here, though,' said the mother, 'the question doesn't seem to me to arise.'

'Oh, no!' said the girl, 'of course not. Not in a straight gaff with one girl, no. But if the place is crooked with a few of them, and the agent knows it and he takes money from the girl, then the law says he's a brothel-keeper even though he's not the landlord.'

'But not if he takes it from the man.'

'No, Mum.'

'Then we do have our uses,' Frankie said.

The women both smiled politely and a bit impatiently.

'All the same,' the old Mum said, 'I should say with the new laws making it difficult for the girls out on the streets, the crooked landlords are going to play an even bigger part than they used to do before.'

'Naturally. And you know, Mum, it's a funny thing. In the old days on the streets, in spite of all you read of in the Sundays, the business wasn't really organized to all that great extent. Among the foreign girls, yes, maybe, but most of our girls just did their own deals with the landlords. But now, with the question of rooms becoming so important, I shouldn't be surprised to see that kind of an estate-agent, and the hospitality bureaus and such, moving in on the thing in a very much bigger way.'

'That's the trouble about laws,' the mother said, pouring another great gurgling cup of tea. Her daughter continued,

'The people who pass them just don't know a thing first hand, and when they set out to alter things for the better as they call it, they end up by making them far worse. Now, take the game. Up till a year ago, it was broadly speaking single operators, single girls. Now it's going to be big business, and go all commercial. But there you are. Here in England they think that if a thing goes on behind closed doors, it's better. In fact though, as we're going to see, it's worse. I mean different, anyway.' The girl sipped ruminatively. 'I wonder,' she said, 'why they don't just leave us alone. Why it is they hate us so.'

'It's not you they hate,' Frankie said, 'it's us—and I'll tell you why?'

The two women turned and eyed him as do adults when a bright child who's overheard an adult conversation chips in with a remark that will be possibly idiotic, possibly cute, and just possibly the revelation of an infant wisdom.

'They hate us,' said Frankie, 'so far as I can see for three reasons —possibly more I haven't thought of.'

Mild curiosity sat in four female eyes.

'They *don't* hate us,' Frankie said, 'because we're wicked, and they're not.'

The word 'wicked' fell on the air with a slight embarrassment on account, in this setting, of its total irrelevance: as if, on a race-track, a jockey had suddenly implied that any doubt was possible about the value of steeple-chasing.

'Then why do they?' said the girl.

'In the first place,' said Frankie who by now had meditated long and deeply on this theme, 'they hate us because they put their own guilty feelings on our heads.'

'They feel *guilty*?' the Mum said, as if pronouncing an indecent word.

'Some of them do, Mum,' said her daughter. 'As a matter of fact for some of them that's just the kick.'

'In the second place,' Frankie continued, 'they resent having to pay for what we get free.'

'Frankie!' cried the Mum. 'Don't be so vulgar!'

'And in the third,' he went on, 'they're simply jealous of us: cock-jealous, I mean. They know if they did it as well as we do, they wouldn't need to pay a girl at all.'

'You're being disgusting,' said the Mum. But her daughter smiled. 'So now you've got *that* off your chest,' she said, as her Mum cleared away the unharmonious tea-things.

She reached over and put her arms round Frankie and just left them there, so that he felt their weight: the only moment when arms—those busy, utilitarian limbs—seem voluptuous as breasts or thighs. 'You love me, don't you, Frankie dear?' she said.

He kissed her hard and comfortably. 'I don't *love* you,' he said with friendly scorn, 'and you know I don't. But I certainly like you —and your body, well, it's strawberries and cream.'

She laughed and pulled free, though easily, when her Mum returned, in a way Frankie liked because it showed not deference to the mother, but that her physical life with Frankie was their own concern and no one else's, not even Mum's.

'People are funny,' the mother observed sagely, seating her huge self (she was one of those women whose very soul seems in their bottoms) and picking up, though at a tangent, some threads of the earlier conversation. 'When they get an idea they've very often no idea what their real idea behind it is. For instance,' she said, weighing her pendulous elbows on the stalwart table, 'take healing, such as I do. Well, it's not for *healing* in point of actual fact that a great many of them come to see me.' She looked at each of them, as if inviting the real explanation and defying them to utter it. 'They come,' she said, 'simply because they're lonely and want sympathetic company.'

'A lot of mine do, too,' the girl said.

'Oh, I suppose so,' said the Mum.

'That's what the law and watch committees and busybodies generally don't realize. A lot of the clients, if they didn't come to us, would be in mental homes. There's not a girl, among the nicer ones I mean, who's not had the experience of straightening out some kinky character and even maybe, who knows? saving his marriage for him, and his home.'

'That's a new angle,' Frankie said.

'Don't be sarcastic, Frank,' the mother told him.

'All I'm trying to show you, Frankie,' said his girl, 'is that they're just as wrong, often, to hate us as they are to hate men like you.'

'Live and let live,' said the mother, 'is my motto. But as a matter of

fact, so far as the law's concerned I don't think they're unreasonable:
I mean the older more experienced officers. They bear no malice
usually. They just follow the book of rules.'

'Except for the ones that provoke you,' the girl said, 'or frame
you, or try to take advantage of their position, I'd agree with you
more or less.'

'Who does that leave?' said Frankie.

'Oh, quite a lot of them. I've even had clients among the Force,'
the girl said demurely.

'But a lot of them are bent, just like you say,' said Frankie. 'Well,
come to think of it, don't they *have* to be? I don't mean the station-
sergeants, or the men on the beat who help old ladies across zebras,
but the bright boys, the vice people, the CID. I just ask you this:
how can they possibly catch real criminals unless they understand
what goes on in their minds?'

The women gazed at him as he uttered this subversive thought.

'So far as I can see,' said Frankie, 'the coppers are simply criminals who don't happen to *commit* crimes—not usually, anyway—
because their graft, their occupation, is not that but to *detect* them.
But they've got the criminal mentality all right. Well, I mean: just
take a look at some of their faces, specially the eyes! And those bodies!
All sticking out in awkward, unexpected places—so peculiar!'

'I think you're exaggerating,' the mother said, after a pause.

'Oh, sure!' said Frankie. 'And besides, I've no experience, you may
say. Why! Think of it! I haven't even been inside the nick yet,
except for those nautical little episodes in foreign parts . . .'

'Now, now, dear,' his girl said gently.

'Don't get me wrong!' said Frankie, who was beginning to feel
that most delicious of intoxications, the excitement of an *idea*, and
like all drunkards cared less and less, as it inspired him, whether his
audience was also drunk, or no. 'I'm not against coppers like some
people are. I don't hate them or anything—not at all: why bother?
All I say is they *are* like that, they're bound to be like that, and
what's wrong with the set-up in this country is not what *they* are,
but what all the mugs *think* they are: because the facts about them
aren't generally understood and, anyway, most people just don't
want to *know*.'

'And *why* don't they?' asked, or rather said, the Mum.

'Because they're all like you, dear. Comfortable clots.'

'Well!'

'Frankie!'

'Well?'

All three had risen. The Mum, with great 'dignity', collected up the bits-and-pieces women always have on such occasions (no sweeping, decisive female exit is possible without stage props—*and* the implication that if not expeditiously collected, the offending male will add injury to insult by purloining them), and made off, escorted to the balcony by her daughter, where one of those feminine duos could be heard in which both speak at once yet each absolutely understands the other. Frankie sat on the table, hands in his pockets, marshalling his forces for the ensuing row.

But it burst with the mutes on, all in undertones. The girl just looked at him, sighed a bit and said, 'I know you don't like her, Frankie, but after all she is my Mum and she's bloody useful to us.'

'I agree with every word you say.'

'Well, dear?'

Frankie took her in his arms. 'Are you *sure* she's your Mum?' he said. 'I can't imagine how an old cow like that gave birth to you.'

'I haven't seen *your* Ma ever, don't forget.'

'You'll meet her in paradise. Not here.'

'Oh? I didn't know. Well, dear, there it is. If you want to alter the arrangement say so, but we can't have little scenes like that too frequently.'

'No.' Frankie looked into her eyes affectionately and with profound but uncritical mistrust. 'You know what you're doing to me?' he said. 'I'll tell you: you're blackmailing me.'

'Over this?'

'Over everything. The threat's always there. Take it and like it, boy, or else.'

'You think so?'

'Naturally. In the game the woman picks the man, whatever he may think, and holds him not with money but with blackmail.'

'Not me. You're free to go, dear, and there'll be no come-backs. I don't want you to, you know that, but you're free.'

'Me? Are you kidding? Not in this set-up, baby—never. Once you're in you can't escape—not because of the loot, or even because

of the law, but because if you like the girl a lot, as I do, then you're
really hooked.'

'Well? And so?'

'Well, it's just frightening a bit, girl, that's all. Because so long as
you like *me* it's all okay—but if one day you didn't! Or if you really
lost *your* temper with me!'

'I never do. Not often, anyway.'

'Or we both got high, filled up with lush, and raised our voices!'

'That could happen, I suppose . . .'

'Or if I fell for someone else, or *you* did maybe, and you knew,
and I didn't know! That would be most dangerous of all!'

They were still holding each other, firm but loose, smiling a little
as they spoke. 'You know, dear,' she said, 'this conversation has
come up between every ponce and every whore at some time or
another, and in some form or other—all I wonder is that we've not
got around to having it before.'

'You're a Jezebel,' he said.

'Oh, no. No, no, I'm square and solid, quite a trusty. But: dig this,
Frank, and there's no escaping it. A whore can do without a ponce
if it has to be that way: but a ponce can never do without a whore—
not ever.'

'Dig.'

'That's just the situation, baby. So what you say?'

'What I say is, darling, that I'm going to rape you. Take all that
off and come on in.'

MR LOVE (STILL)

WHEN he left her sleeping, Frankie gathered in the dark some
minimal possessions plus twenty pounds from the laundry-basket
(where petty-cash was kept, loose under the week's linen, so that a
pound note had once been sent, in error, to the laundry (and returned!)), and he walked out into the Kilburn dawn. He set off
across the city at an angle to the west–east, north–south pattern of
its thoroughfares and, as dawn broke, he arrived again at Stepney.

Frankie's real objection to his situation was not really any of those that had come up last evening in discussion with his girl. His objection was that, in a general way, the man–woman relationship was taking a wrong and insupportable form. Among seamen there still survives from earlier days of masculine domination the notion that the man, at least in appearances, wears the slacks; and that the woman is she who sighs at the mariner's departure and accepts, without too much question, the equally sighing wife-in-every-port. On land, in England, he'd found that the symbol of the husband was now that dreadful little twerp you saw on hoardings who wore a woman's apron while he did, alone, the washing-up. This conception would have been just as repellent to Frankie in a legitimate marriage as in any unmarried-husband-and-wife connection.

And yet he would miss his girl—and really her. In Frankie's life sexual exchange was a very serious business, and he was old enough to have discovered that contrarily to all the legends about the delights of promiscuity, if you were really good at it yourself and found a woman who enhanced your sexual splendour—and her own —this was a rare thing to be clung to and protected. She'd certainly, in this way, got in well under his skin; and no thought of her clients had disturbed his raptures. Partly, because that core of herself which she kept absolutely intact throughout all her commercial encounters was fired to greater heat by the very fact that she held it, in reserve, entirely for him. Partly, because the idea that other men coveted her was far from diminishing her attraction to him: an instinct which, when one comes to think of it, is also shared in many cases by the clients of prostitutes themselves, and also, it may be, by complaisant husbands of candidly unfaithful wives.

Stepney, in early morning, has a macabre, poetic beauty. It is one of those areas of London that is thoroughly confused about itself, being in transition from various ancient states of being to new ones it is still busy searching for. The City, which still preserves its Roman quality of ending very abruptly at its ancient gates, towers beyond Aldgate pump, then stops: so that gruesome Venetian financial palaces abut on to semi-slums. From the dowdy baroque of Liverpool street station, smoke and thunder fall on Spitalfields market with its vigorous dawn life and odour of veg, fruit and flowers— like blended essences of the citizens' duties, delights and fantasies. Below the windowless brick warehouses of the Port of London

Authority, the road life of Wentworth street—almost unknown elsewhere in London where roads are considered means by which you
move from place to place, not places in themselves—bubbles, over-
spills and sways in argument and shrill persuasion, to the off-stage
squawks of thousands of slaughtered chickens. Old Montague
street with its doorless shops that open outward in the narrow
thoroughfare, and its discreet, secretive synagogues, has still the
flavour of a semi-voluntary ghetto. Further south, in Commercial
road, are the nocturnal vice caffs that members of parliament and of
Royal Commissions are wont to visit, invariably accompanied by a
detective-inspector to ensure that their expedition will reveal nothing characteristic of the area; and which, when suppressed, pop up
again immediately elsewhere or under different names with different
men of straw at the identical old address. In Cable street, below, the
castaways from Africa and the Caribbean perform a perpetual,
melancholy, wryly humorous ballet of which they are themselves
the only audience. Amid incredible slums—which, one may imagine,
with the huge new blocks replacing them, are preserved there by
authority to demonstrate the contrast of before-and-after—are pieces
of railway architecture of grimly sombre grandeur. Then come the
docks with masts and funnels strangely emerging above chimney-
tops, and house-locked basins, the entry to which by narrow canals
and swinging bridges seems, to the landsman, an impossibility, were
it not for the cargo boats nestling snugly between the derelict tene-
ments. Suddenly, beyond this, you come upon the river: which this
far down, lined with wharves and cranes and bearing great ocean-
loving steamers, is no longer the pretty, grubby, playground of the
higher reaches but already, by now, the sea.

A great charm of the area is that only here, in one sense, is London
really a capital city at all. For what, elsewhere in the world, dis-
tinguishes capitals from their bleak provincial brethren is that
they're open for business all night, and for seven days in the week.
Thanks to the markets, seamen, and Commonwealth minorities, in
Stepney you can eat and drink, as well as other things, at any hour
you choose to; and thanks to the alternation of the Jewish sabbath
with the Gentile, the shops and markets never close. All that remains astonishing, since this is England, about this delightful state
of affairs is that no one has yet managed to suppress it.

Frankie breakfasted in Stepney at one of those cafés usually conducted by Somalis which, unlike the more exclusive Maltese, Asian, or Caribbean establishments, are often neutral ground for clients of the most diverse nationalities. And so fell into conversation with a Glaswegian seaman, whose opening shot was to announce that he'd just come out of the nick. Observing the etiquette on these occasions, Frankie didn't ask for what and offered the mariner ten bob. This he accepted as by right. For the announcement of a recent release from prison, like that by children who tell you it's their birthday, is intended to provoke an instant, identical reaction, the scale of the subsidy varying with the degree of the donor's affluence and of intimacy, if any, with the uncaged bird.

'Yes,' said the Scot—speaking in those particular tones Scots use which suggest, with incredible self-esteem and unction (based, it would seem, on nothing very tangible), that each of their platitudes and banalities has a prodigious sagacity and savour—'it was all on account of a Salvation Army laddie.'

Frankie, whom the man bored already, expressed polite surprise.

'He came into a boozer,' the Scot continued, 'where I was partaking of a dram, and he shook his collecting-box underneath my nose, appealing to me and my mates that we should exercise a bit of self-denial.'

The Hebridian fixed his leery, bleary eyes on Frankie, who courteously raised his brows.

'Self-denial!' the Scot repeated. 'So I said to him this: that his coming into pubs where men went precisely to escape from hypocrites like him, and blackmailing everybody under the protection of his self-appointed uniform, was a form of spiritual pride which—as any Presbyterian can tell you—is the deadliest sin of all, and that his first task for the salvation of his own soul by blood and fire was to deny himself this hideous satisfaction.'

'Ah,' Frankie said.

'Whereupon,' the Scot continued, emphasizing each word as if it fell from his lips like newly minted coin, 'the Sassenachs in the boozer, one and all, took this man's side against me because the English, you see—excuse me, my very good friend—haven't the courage of their convictions and none of them, except for me, would dare to say the man was a damned imposter.'

'And so?' Frankie said.

'An argument—a fight—knocked off—the courts—previous convictions—two months—no remission.'

'Who pinched you?' Frankie asked.

'Plain-clothes. In a plain car. You know? One of those ordinary vehicles that are not quite what they seem.'

'Crafty.'

'Ah, well ... not really so. Just, man, that I, on this particular occasion, being intoxicated was *not*.'

'And now what? Back to sea?'

'No: back for a wee spell to Glasgow. I've had an offer of a ship but me, after this experience, I must have a wee spell at hame in Bonnie Scotland ...'

Into his tone and eyes had come dollops of the atrocious sentimentality that so frequently lies below the granite surface of the hard-headed Scot.

'Who's using the berth?'

'Who can tell? Why, man—you want it? Well, if you've got a tenner for the quartermaster and no one's preceded you in search of it, take this address and so forth and send me a post-card from the Argentine.'

He handed to Frankie a cigarette-wrapping inscribed with critical particulars, and Frankie thanked him and immediately took his leave. For he was certain—not being at all a fool—that if he didn't get out of England in a day or two he'd return, just as certainly, to Kilburn.

As he walked through Stepney, he passed by the all-night caffs that cater for the exhibitionist dregs of the vice trade and where, in the morning, a few survivors from the last night's market-place remained: either disappointed hustlers of both sexes who'd failed to connect and slept there, or dissatisfied clients who'd returned from various squalid set-ups whither their earlier imaginings had lured them not to complain (for this was useless: and who to complain to?), but as the beast returns from the smaller, empty water-hole to the larger. Among them was a sprinkling of the different, morning clientele: lorry-drivers, local workers and a few from the West of the city who'd visited the gamble-houses and called in for breakfast to count (mentally) their losses or more unlikely gains. It is at this hour, when someone sleepy is sweeping out among this driftwood, and not in the hopeful afternoon or the intoxicated evening, that moralists should paint their portraits of Gin Lane.

But for Frankie the change was that everything he'd seen earlier in these places now fell into focus. Just as a veteran, seeing soldiers drilling, finds no more mystery in their gyrations, so did Frankie recall this incident, or that person, which had seemed inexplicable but now no longer were. 'What you got in that bag?' a voice asked him sharply.

A copper was blocking the morning view: and worse still, disturbing Frankie's tranquil train of troubled thought. 'You want to have a look?' he said, dumping the bag down at the officer's highly polished feet.

'Open up,' said the officer.

Frankie bent casually, unzipped the zip and straightened himself remotely, leaving the bag still closed.

'I said open up.'

Frankie surveyed the copper, eyes to eyes. Unlike all but a fraction of the citizenry he did not fear coppers in the least: feared, perhaps, any damage, physical or worse, they might inflict on him, but not them as men at all. Nor was he in the least impressed by the art coppers have in a sudden crisis of calling up childhood memories, and suggesting to the accused that they are the father and the person they interrogate abruptly the child who, even if he hasn't broken something, feels he must have. So for a moment, there was an impasse: for the copper was young and not quite sure of the precedents in his predicament. Till Frankie, in a somewhat equivocal gesture of compromise, put a foot on one end of the hold-all which caused the other end to gape wide open, revealing his guiltless clothes.

'What's these?' said the officer.

Frankie made no reply. The officer inclined himself and rummaged. 'Are they yours?' he said, looking up.

Frankie nodded.

'I asked you a question,' said the officer.

'Yes. I heard you. And I gave you an answer.'

The officer, his decision made, stood up. 'I'm not satisfied with all this,' he said. 'I want you to come along to the station.'

Frankie zipped up the bag, lifted it and said, 'Are you arresting me?'

'I didn't say that. I said—'

'If you're not arresting me you know there's no charge to bring; and to take me to the station's just a bit of spite.'

The copper took Frankie's arm, text-book fashion. 'So you think you *are* arresting me,' Frankie said.

The officer applied the text-book pressure which should have resulted in Frankie's inevitable propulsion along the road—but somehow, he didn't move. 'You're coming in,' said the officer, heaving desperately, 'for resisting an officer in the execution of his duties as well as the other thing.'

Frankie laughed out loud. 'What other thing?' he cried.

'Come on!' cried the officer, giving a colossal shove.

Abruptly, Frankie started walking smartly forward so that the officer was now dragged behind his prisoner as is a dog-lover by a Great Dane. Round a corner Frankie stopped abruptly, making his custodian slightly overshoot him, and said, 'Son, do you really have to do this to a merchant seaman about his lawful business?'

'Is that what you say you are?' said the officer, panting.

'It's all I know, son, the sea. It's all I am and ever hope to be.'

'Oh, yes?' said the young copper, schooled in scepticism. 'Well, I don't think so. As a matter of fact,' he added with a penetrating professional stare, 'we know all about you . . .'

Despite a momentary throb, Frankie's good sense told him he could utterly ignore this classical copper's gambit. 'I'll tell you something, son,' he said, 'about you and your little lot. You *do* know secrets about people, yes: but the secrets you know are all secrets of no importance.'

The intrusion of this philosophical theme was greatly to the young officer's distaste. He searched in vain for a helpful colleague or even a law-abiding citizen, and realized that now his disagreeable choice lay between a fight or of letting, or appearing to let, Frankie escape: both detrimental to the junior constable's estimate of his dignity.

A voice said, 'Having a bit of trouble?' It was that of an older officer who had emerged from a scrap-metal yard where he had been passing the time of morning. 'This feller's awkward,' said the

junior officer, giving Frankie an authoritative shake. Four hands—
which, compared with two, are not as twofold but as twentyfold or
more—now seized on Frankie and hustled him stationwards. The
early hour, from the officers' point of view, could not have been
more convenient: for Frankie was comfortably in time for the morning convoy to the magistrate's court. The old boy—one of the
vanishing type whose sagacious sallies are still reported in the inside
bottom columns of the evening papers—gave Frankie the option of
forty shillings or of seven days. When asked if he had anything to
say, Frankie remarked in a casual and reasoned tone: 'If the law
takes a man in for nothing, he may decide he might as well get
taken in for something.' The magistrate nodded, made no direct
comment, and withdrew the option of a fine.

MR LOVE AND MR JUSTICE

THE attraction of wrestling is not so much the sport itself (if it
be one), as in the survivals it enshrines of ancient customs. If anyone
wants to know what an old Music Hall audience was like (when
gallery boys hurled pease puddings and pigs' trotters over the
cowering heads of the grilled-in musicians on to the performers), or
going back a bit, what a bear-baiting public may have resembled, or
further still, the spectators of a gladiatorial show—he may probably
capture some of their atmospheres at a wrestling match. The
audience, indeed, are much more arresting than the fighters: the
faces of mild respectable men in business suits are twisted into
vicious snarls, those of women, shrieking violent obscenities, wear
masks of gloating ferocious glee. The bouts themselves seem to fall
into two categories: comparatively straight matches of incompar-
able boredom in which huge hunks of living meat lie locked in
painful and contorted postures; and then the 'villain-and-hero'
bouts, sorts of popular moralities, wherein one wrestler becomes,
presumably by pre-arrangement, St. George, and the other (usually
the more polished performer) the odious dragon. It is a tribute to
the artistry of these thespian practitioners of grunt-and-groan that

though all but the dimmest-witted of the audience know the performance is a fake—or, one might say, an allegory—they accept the convention of this Jack-the-Giant-killer world entirely. So that when Jack, attacked basely from the rear by the treacherous giant who just a second ago was pleading on his quavering knees for mercy, outwits the monster and hurls him four feet high and six feet wide with a resounding crash on to the groaning mat, the audience yells the applause that may have greeted David as he returned from his encounter with Goliath.

Among the spectators of the bout between Boris the Bulgar and the Tasmanian Devil were Frank and his girl, now reconciled and firmly reunited and comfortably ensconced in ringside seats; and also among those present in ringsides likewise (complimentaries, in this case) were the newly installed tenants of their Kilburn flat, Edward and his beloved woman. Surrounding them was a cross-section of that part of the London populace which is rarely to be seen elsewhere (except at race meetings, certain East and South London pubs, and courts and jails), and whose chief characteristics are their uninhibited violence, their heartless bonhomie, and their total rejection alike of the left-ish Welfare State and the right-ish Property-owning democracy: a sort of Jacobean underground movement in the age of planned respectability from grave to cradle.

Up in the ring it was Boris the Bulgar (need one say?) who was cast for the role of villain. He was short, squat, bald and lithe, and probably hailed from Canning Town or Newington Butts. His face, if such one could call it, wore a built-in scowl when all was in his favour, a contortion of dreadful agony when his opponent secured a grip, and a look of abject ignominy when fortune momentarily failed to smile upon him. With the referee (a huge, sandy, mild-eyed man of tough but exquisite manners) he was on the worst of terms, perpetually disputing his decisions; and with the crowd even more so for he hurled back, in reply to their hoots and screams, base insults by voice and scandalous gesture. What a contrast was the Tasmanian Devil! A large, sad, slow-moving man whose whole bent, bruised body suggested a life of unjust suffering dedicated, much more in sorrow than in anger, to a resigned forgiveness of the world's worst treacheries and wrongs. How often did the Devil not break away, voluntarily, and release his victim from an impossible posture, chivalrously to show that even an animal so base must be given yet another chance! How obedient he was to the least remonstrance of the wise and patient referee! And how earnestly he looked up at the audience, apologizing with a wry smile for any faulty manoeuvre that had caused him untold agonies at the Bulgar's hands, shrugging sadly his red and massive shoulders at some outrageous piece of wickedness of his adversary, and occasionally, the fierce light of battle appearing in his brow-locked eyes, appealing to the masses as he held the atrocious Bulgar at his mercy for *their* impartial judgment (free from the prejudices that momentarily marred his own) to decide the exact nature of Boris's so richly merited fate.

This sealed, between contests and amid the patrons' recapitulative buzz, Edward's girl squeezes his hand and moved her hips even closer to his off-duty gaberdine. But Edward was staring into space. 'It ought to be suppressed,' he said.

'What ought, dear?' she said, surprised.

'All this,' said Edward, frowning. 'It's a disgrace.'

'But I thought you liked it.'

He looked round at her. 'Oh, yes, well I do: I mean the fight. But it's the audience I'm speaking of. I've seen more wanted men in here this evening than any day in the line-up. *And* flashing their money about—somebody's money, anyway.'

'They've got to go somewhere . . .' she suggested.

'I know where they all ought to go . . .'

She squeezed him again. 'Well, don't complain too much,' she said. 'You're doing a bit better yourself since you got your danger money.'

'Mustn't talk shop here, dear,' he said softly.

'Oh, I'm sorry. I liked the Tasmanian one, Edward. I think he was sexy.'

'That hunk of meat? Well, that's what the whole thing's meant for, I suppose. I notice there's nearly as many women here as men . . .'

'Oh yes, we love it! Those big men tied in knots!'

'Lovers' knots.'

'Oh, Ted! You can be so crude!'

A stir in the audience, and the incomprehensive barking from the man in a hired tuxedo at the mike, both heralded the next pair of

warriors. Frankie looked round expectantly, but his girl chewed her
cashew nuts in silence. 'Stay for this one, babe,' he said.

'Okay, Frankie, if you say so, but never again. It's such a drag.'

'This will be better: younger fellers, more your type.'

'No wrestler's my type. They all look like blown-up balloons. Me,
I like lean men.'

'Skinny like me?'

'You're not skinny—not since you've been with me, anyway.'

'Not in here, darling. Watch what you say . . .'

' "Been with me". What's wrong with that? And Frankie, just look
at the audience! All those old bitches: I bet they've not had a man
in years—apart from hubby.'

'What's wrong with hubby? Look! Here they both come—young
kiddies, like I said.'

'Yeah?' The girl scanned them casually. 'I'll wait till they get their
gowns off,' she said, 'before I pronounce judgment.'

'It'll be a real fight,' said Frankie. 'There's nothing to beat a fight
between two young men, provided they're reasonably matched.'

'You think they will be—in a place like this? Listen, Frankie.
There's only one kind of fight I like, and that's with you on a six-
foot divan.'

'This'll give you an appetite,' said Frankie.

By the unexacting standards of the grunt-and-groan game, the
fight seemed to be a fair one. At any rate, plenty of things happened
that surely no one could possibly have predetermined or predicted.
When the two men bounced individually off the ropes to gain
momentum, they collided and knocked each other out (apparently).
At one moment a wrestler was sitting *on* the other's head, though
this man was standing, and contrived to remain there for at least
forty seconds. And at another, when one man staggered in dazed
pain this may have been simulated, but hardly the sudden gesture of
concern with which the man who'd hurt him ran up and stroked his
arm. As the fight developed, two distinct personalities emerged.
One fighter would attack sharply, and even when his hold seemed
powerful and secure he'd break away abruptly, of his own accord,
to mount a different, unexpected hostile manoeuvre. The other, in
sharp comparison with the two earlier wrestlers whose expressions
in combat had been perpetually bestial, wore a certain grace and

freedom in the savagery of his face. When they were locked tight it was often quite impossible to tell, at moments, who was who and which limbs belonged to which: though the different coloured shorts they wore were something of an indication. The nicest thing about them both—and professionally the most convincing—was their apparent indifference to the audience around them to whom they paid little or no court, entirely intent on battle. The bout, which lasted (most unusual in wrestling) all its rounds, seemed inconclusive, although the referee did raise one tired arm: by the audience this was of course disputed, but rather languidly, as the fight had been too good for them to enjoy it.

At the interval most patrons went out in the long bars for some solid boozing. Criminal aristocrats, all wearing hats (they looked as if they wore them in their baths, beds and tombs), stood in little squares to talk so that there was no direction from which a stranger might approach the party unobserved. Women of hideous splendour —looking like actresses in a banned play who'd strayed outside the pass-door a moment—stood absolutely motionless with a gin glass, ignoring their escorts and ignored by them. The wrestlers of the earlier bout appeared in mufti, but betrayed by squashed ears and colossal shoulders, to have a quick one and talk contracts with alarming men who never blinked and spoke with a fraction of their mouths in voices inaudible from more than eighteen inches.

Frankie and Edward glanced at each other, their eyes locked, held for a second then fell away. Then each, as men do to assess a man, looked at the other's woman, and across both their faces there passed a flicker of slight disdain.

MR JUSTICE

A CHANGE in the laws does not fundamentally affect a copper's work: the only things that could do that are profound social and political changes, or (if such a thing, in mid-twentieth-century England, is conceivable) essential religious changes—not just of fashion (which happen so frequently and meaninglessly) but of basic form. Otherwise, if the moral structure of the nation does not alter, a change of its laws means merely, for the Force, a modification of its tactics, not its strategy (nor of its very self): the same crimes remain and the same criminals, but merely operate in different ways which have to be anticipated and assailed with fresh techniques.

This was the reason for a 'conference' (as he called his staff meetings) in the Detective-sergeant's office. There were present the star sleuth, Edward Justice, a plain-clothes copperess and one civilian: or rather, a hybrid creature—a former copper, now retired from the Force, who'd gone into business (quadrupling his income) as a private detective, while still (very naturally) maintaining his contacts among his former comrades who (knowing that only death could sunder one of their kind for ever from his calling) were prepared to trust—and use—him up to a certain point.

The Detective-sergeant addressed the little group. 'The problem as I see it 's this,' he said. 'We've got to crack down on the Madams. More and more of these girls are going on the phone, and it's the Madams who are picking out the best earners among them and organizing these high-grade semi-brothels. They're crafty, of course. There's no girls *living* on the premises, and they change them round so much, by calling them on the blower for a particular appointment with a client, that it's hard to log their visits if you keep watch —and play it straight, of course—to get the necessary number for a prosecution. Then there's the clients, too. The particular Madam we've chosen as our trial target seems to specialize in the bowler hat and rolled umbrella category, mostly elderly and—from the enquiries we've already made—the sort of mug you have to handle carefully, as they've got connections. So that's why,' the Detective-sergeant continued, eyeing the ex-copper detective with a friendly, mocking air, 'we've thought of enlisting the aid and assistance of our friend here.'

They all looked at the semi-civilian who smiled and said, 'Always happy to help you beginners out of your predicaments.'

'Now, here's the plan,' said the Detective-sergeant after a wry, polite, and not very pleasant smile. 'It's a three-pronged attack, as you'll see. Number one, we keep watch in the routine manner, naturally, and for that we'll be using the bread-delivery van.'

There was a muffled groan.

'Yes?' said the Detective-sergeant sharply.

'Sir,' someone said. 'If that van of ours keeps breaking down on bread rounds in every suspect street in north-west London, won't someone soon start to rumble us?'

'It's all we've got,' the Detective-sergeant said severely: as with so many strategists, 'the plan' already was, for him, a reality to which reality itself must needs conform; besides which—as he was scarcely able to divulge—the watchers outside were not really one of his 'prongs' at all, but were intended to serve as a decoy to the sharp-eyed Madam who, he hoped, would imagine them to be her only danger.

'The second attack,' said the Detective-sergeant, 'will be from this lassie here'—and he indicated with a sexy but official leer the horse-faced copperess who sat primly on her kitchen chair, showing a regulation inchage of her bony and well-exercised legs. 'Her task will be to follow the girls home, try to locate their addresses, if possible identify their ponces and—well, I wouldn't put it past so experienced an officer—get on friendly terms with them.'

There were discreet and cordial chortles, and the copperess, smiling slightly, showed her teeth in a grimace that hinted this feat was far from being beyond her professional (and womanly) competence.

'There's only one thing,' said the star sleuth, who hitherto had maintained an aloof and almost disdainful silence.

'Well?'

'I've checked on one or two,' he said, 'and this Madam's got a thing about using girls whose ponces we'd find it difficult to get at.'

'Lesbian girls?' said the ex-copper detective.

The star sleuth nodded.

'Yes, that's a difficulty,' the ex-officer said. 'You can get them for procuring if you're lucky, but with a living on immoral earnings charge, juries just wouldn't understand the situation. Even magistrates are sometimes a bit slow to grasp it.'

'Also,' the star sleuth continued, 'there's one girl, I know, who's shacked up with a teenager: and you realize how hard it is to pin a thing like that on one of them.'

'These teenagers!' said the ex-copper, sighing. 'They're a caution!'

The Detective-sergeant broke in with some vexation. 'I've considered these various angles,' he said, 'and as for you'—and he pointed a blunt index in the star sleuth's direction—'I hope your private investigations haven't buggered up the situation prematurely.'

The copperess looked at the varnished ceiling. 'Oh, pardon,' the Detective-sergeant said. 'It's still hard, after all these years, to remember we have ladies in the Force.' He gave her a cracked grin, and proceeded: 'So—attack number three: the place itself: and that's where our friend here (smile at the ex-copper) comes into the picture. Perhaps, then, you'd just tell these young officers in your own words the essential gist of our earlier private conversation.'

The ex-cop, his moment come, beamed with the bonhomie of someone who knows all the inner secrets but is freed from the servitude demanded to acquire them.

'As I see the picture,' he explained, 'I'm a randy guinea-pig.'

He paused for effect: but the laughter coming from the gallery, not the stalls or circle, he continued—suddenly very grave—'The spiel is this. I'm a client—yes? I've got her phone number, and I've got the name of a kosher client that you pinched for parking as my alleged sponsor, so my call to the premises won't seem untoward. I get in the place on several occasions, over a period of time, until I know the set-up in all its aspects and we're ready for the raid. When that comes—well, I'm the Roman legionary inside the Trojan horse.'

'We won't ask,' said the Detective-sergeant gaily, 'what, apart from your duties, you actually *do* in there.'

'Oh, I should think not! My report on *that* part of the business is strictly private for my missus.'

'Any questions?' said the Detective-sergeant.

After the traditional pause, the star sleuth said, 'So we don't touch the clients?'

'Not at all. Strictly not at all.'

'You'll excuse me, sir,' said the star sleuth very deferentially, 'but I do think there's one reason why you should consider it. It's this. They're the weak link. They're not doing anything illegal, as we know, like the girls and Madam are, but unlike them they're mugs, after all, and have their *respectability* to consider. And when a man's attached to that I've always found he'll talk with very little persuasion.'

'They're not guilty of anything,' said the ex-copper.

'I know that: I've just said so. But don't forget, sir. You can always *arouse* a sense of guilt, especially in a respectable man. Almost everyone feels guilty about *some*thing. And you can work on that.'

'All a bit over my head,' said the Detective-sergeant nastily. 'The orders are as I said. Anything else?'

Edward Justice said, 'Sir: what about the lawyers?'

'What lawyers? I don't get it, sonny.'

Edward looked round, feeling a lot of eyes on him, gulped, and said, 'These girls, sir, some of them, are earning several hundreds untaxed every week—they or their ponces are, I mean. And this Madam, sir, she must have a fabulous income and I dare say she'll try to protect them to a certain extent. Well, sir, if they're raided that means lawyers—big ones. And all I wanted to ask was, what the procedure in the event of arrest should be.'

Like so many young men new to a business, Edward had committed the solecism of asking a highly intelligent question that it was not appropriate he should ask, for several reasons. Firstly, because that wasn't what the particular briefing was about: one thing at a time in the Force as anywhere else. Next, because the whole subject of the triangle of criminal, copper and the courts is so intricate, practically and philosophically, that it can't possibly be explained in a short answer. Thirdly, there were aspects of this relationship so delicate that they have, in the Force, to be learned by experience rather than taught specifically.

The Detective-sergeant, eyeing Edward and remembering his own young days, said quite kindly, 'The procedure, constable, is as laid down: just follow that.'

'All I wanted to get at, sir,' said Edward, feeling from the slight electricity in the atmosphere he was 'on to' something and unable to resist the risk of burning his fingers on it, 'was this. When we detain them, how long do we keep them before we let them see their lawyers?'

The Detective-sergeant looked at him hard. 'As long as the book allows,' he said. 'Any further questions?'

There were none, and the little group dispersed. The ex-copper wanted to stay and chat the Detective-sergeant but this officer, exercising the privilege of an active if junior rank to a retired even if formerly senior colleague, turfed him politely out, detaining Edward. 'Sit down, son,' he said, 'I want to talk to you.'

The Detective-sergeant lit his pipe and said, 'Your question was quite all right, lad, but it wasn't quite the time and place to ask it. Now as for lawyers we have them too, you know, as well as anyone else; they're very good ones, believe me, and in the more important cases we get the services of the top brains in the land.'

'Yes, sir,' said Edward.

'I see, of course, the point you were getting at and I don't object at all to you considering it. A good man in the Force like I believe you to be—or getting to be with time—very naturally wants to secure a conviction if he can. That's what we're here for, after all; it's our duty to the profession and, if you like to put it that way, to society at large. We have also, of course, certain rules and regulations as to how you can get a man convicted—and as to how you can't—drawn up I don't know by who and don't much care because there they are, they exist, they've got to be observed.'

'Yes, sir.'

'*Observed* I said, mark you. But not necessarily, always, in every case to be *obeyed*.'

Here the Detective-sergeant stopped, removed his pipe and contemplated Edward in a fatherly way.

'But the point you've got to grasp,' he continued, 'is this one. If you knock a man off and don't follow the book and get a conviction, and no one asks any questions—then, well and good. And if you do it often enough you'll probably get quick promotion. On the other hand if you chance your arm and do something that's not in the book of rules and come unstuck in court or elsewhere, please don't expect anyone to protect you or excuse you; not me or anyone else, and I want to make that perfectly clear.'

'I understand, sir,' Edward said.

'I hope so. Now, about the particular question that you asked. Obviously, as I need hardly tell you, the longer you can keep a prisoner from his lawyer the better it's likely to be for your particular purposes. Most cases, in my experience, are lost or won in the first hour of the arrest—or at any rate in the first twenty-four of them. If you can keep the lawyers away from him in this critical period your battle's already more than half way over.'

'I see, sir. But . . . well, sir. If he *asks* to see his lawyer? What do you do then?'

'Come now, boy, that's up to you! Don't ask me to *be* your brains on top of everything else . . . It depends on the man, the case, the circumstances—everything! Remember the book—remember the case—and use your judgment. To give you a simple instance. Take formally preferring a charge or warning the person that anything he says will be taken down, etcetera. Well! How many cases couldn't I tell you of when I haven't bothered to do either! In the matter of the charge, you often don't know what it's going to be until you've talked to him quite a bit. And as for the warning . . . well frankly, in most cases I've simply forgotten it—I mean *forgotten* it—and there's no possible come-back there, because no one outside the Force believes that we *don't* warn them. They believe we do just like they believe we wear helmets in our sleep and can tell them the correct time without looking at our watches.'

'Yes, sir, I see.'

'I'd sum it up like this. If you're a good copper, I mean both as a man and an officer, more or less and allowing for human failings, and you're alone in a cell with a man who you know for certain is evil and anti-social, well, you must establish your moral right to prepare him for punishment as best you can. That, in my experience, is usually what the situation is: him and you: very simple, really. There are those who believe (and the Detective-sergeant glanced towards the door whence the others had departed) and who'll tell you a really good copper, professionally speaking I mean, has no conscience: can't afford to have one, or something. Well, there are wiser heads than mine in the Force, and admitted, I've stuck hitherto at Detective-sergeant. But all the same my personal conviction is that it's untrue. To be a good copper, in any sense of the word, you've got to have *certain* basic principles and stick to them.'

'Yes, sir.'

'Good. Now hop it, sonny, I've got work to do.'

When Edward was at the door, however, the Detective-sergeant said to him, 'That girl of yours, by the way. Any developments?'

Edward blushed, and hoped the reasons for it would be mistaken. 'I think things are working out, sir,' he said. 'I'm bringing her gradually round.'

'Ah. Just another thing: perhaps I shouldn't tell you this, but I will. One of our colleagues—I leave to your imagination who—has told me—unofficially, if such a thing exists—you've set up house already with the lady.'

Edward said nothing.

'No objection to that, of course,' the older officer said, 'provided you're just *visiting* her, like, and *not* living as man and wife, and provided I'm *not* formally informed by anyone—I mean in a report —and also provided, I'd say, that, as you tell me, the thing's only temporary and you'll soon be getting wed.'

'Thank you, sir,' Edward said.

'Just watch it, son. That's all.'

'I'd like to thank you, sir,' Edward said again.

The Detective-sergeant smiled. 'No need to: I may need you one day—who knows? That's one of the things about the Force, son, as you've no doubt probably discovered: it's hard to have friends. Mates, yes, dozens of them, and professionally good colleagues, too. But not many you can let yourself confide in.'

MR LOVE

In her warm and chintzy drawing-room the Madam was serving tea and holding court. If a person's identifiable with a locality, her appearance was Kensingtonian: neat, conservative, reliable and uncreative with a hint, perhaps, of the monied leisure of the Bournemouth pines. Her shoes were not smart but clean and dependable, her hair was not permed but well laundered and preserved. The tea-things were of silver, and the biscuits (which nobody took) from a Knightsbridge store. Her tones were quiet and authoritative like those of the chairwoman of a ward caucus; and she was also, if anyone had anything relevant to say, an excellent listener. Her guests were Frankie and his girl, a bisexual prostitute who was one of a team sustaining the sensational decline of a once (and in some senses, still) celebrated Lesbian socialite, and there was also present, like the footman behind the ducal chair, her confidential maid.

'So I think,' Frankie's girl was saying, 'you'll find, as I say, everything will be okay.'

The Madam gazed steadily at Frankie. 'I hope, Frank,' she said, 'you'll not take it amiss I asked your young lady to bring you here to see me, and didn't consider I was asking you to take an unnecessary risk. But the fact is, as I made quite clear to this young girl of yours, that if a girl of mine tells me she has a young man in her life —and I like and expect her to be perfectly frank about who she may be in business with—then before I ask her to help me in my own business here I have to see the young man, or other person in question, to get my own personal impression.'

'Yeah,' Frankie said.

'Frankie didn't very much want to come,' the girl said, smiling at him a little nervously because, about this, there'd been a really prodigious row. 'He took a bit of persuading, I can tell you.'

'That's understandable,' their hostess said.

There was a short pause.

'Look, lady,' Frankie said. 'My girl's here on the work, and it's not in my interest obviously, is it, to stand in her way if she thinks your place is right for her. So I don't object to this interview if it helps matters and provided, if I can say so without offence, it's the only one. There's no need for apologies because I'm not a man who does anything he doesn't want to, and if I agree to anything I don't need thanking for that reason.'

The Madam nodded with reserved approval. The maid looked non-committal, and the bisexual prostitute very dubious.

'This is a select place,' the Madam said, 'and I *mean* select. There are those who think an establishment of this nature has to be noisy, dirty, and generally disreputable. Well, not me or mine. A well-conducted meeting-place such as mine can be every bit as decorous and charming as a hotel is—or ought to be, should I say, because few are as well conducted, though I say so, as my premises.'

'*And* often have more strangers in the bedrooms I dare say,' said Frankie's girl.

The Madam smiled. 'Tea or coffee, with the morning and evening newspapers, are served to all our visitors prior to their departure,' she informed them. 'Is that not so?' she said, suddenly looking over her shoulder at her confidential maid.

'Oh, yes. *And* I press their suits for them, and sometimes wash and dry their socks.'

'Exactly! I set, as a matter of fact, great store by the pleasant character of these departures I've referred to. It's all that happens *after* rather than *before*, in my experience, that determines a satisfied client to return to the establishment again and recommend it to the right sort among his friends.'

'No throwing them out before the milk comes,' said Frankie's girl. The Madam smiled again.

'And what about the law?' asked Frankie. 'You got them fixed?'

His hostess winced slightly and said, 'We take—I and my girls— all necessary measures and precautions. And one of those is to beg someone like yourself, Frank, who's concerned indirectly with my business, to exercise, at all times, a more than usual discretion. Especially, if I may say so, in the matter of conversations other than with, very naturally, your own young lady.'

'Check,' Frankie said.

'They never tap the phones?' Frankie's girl asked, impelled by professional curiosity.

'They're very welcome to,' the Madam answered. 'I, my girls, my dear maid here and, I may say, my clients have trained ourselves to say nothing over the telephone that could, even if recorded, be misinterpreted: I mean, constitute any proof before a court of law. In addition, the firm of solicitors who take my instructions have assured me that, as I expect you know, any evidence of this kind is, legally speaking, inadmissible.'

'So they'll have to fall back on the old tactics,' Frankie said.

'Who?'

'The coppers.'

To everyone but Frankie, the note in the conversation now seemed slightly vulgar.

'So far,' said the Madam with a marked tone of rebuke, 'as the officers of the law are concerned, I need hardly say that one's own common-sense would tell one to say nothing whatever to them without legal counsel. The services of my solicitors, need I tell you, are at the call of any girl whom I employ and who may encounter any difficulties, as much as they are to myself who pay their fees. But there's no special need, I think, for us to anticipate any *special* difficulties. The officers of the law understand my position, just as I understand and respect their own. We have both, after all'—she smiled again—'been on this earth for centuries in one form or another.'

'I wouldn't say that,' said Frankie.

'No?'

'No. Your lot has, of course, as we all know, but from what they taught me at school coppers only came into being a hundred years or so ago.'

'You sure of that, Frankie?' said his girl.

'Well, isn't it right? Sir Robert Peel?'

Frankie's girl was pensive and amazed. 'A time before there were any coppers?' she said. 'I can't believe it.'

'The world,' Frankie said, 'seems to have got on very well for thousands of years without them, and some day I dare say they'll disappear as suddenly as they appeared. We live in the Age of Coppers: but I don't suppose, like anything else, that it'll last for ever.'

The Madam was displeased at such levity. 'I was of course referring,' she said, 'to law enforcement officers who've always existed, I believe, whatever they may have at the time been called. Two ancient institutions are involved: the profession of love, and the enforcement of the laws that govern it.'

'I still think we could do without them,' Frankie said.

The women all raised brows at this typical masculine irresponsibility (or irrelevant intellectual audacity).

'Anyway,' said Frankie, 'they're the only profession, the coppers, who've never had a hero—ever thought of that? They've put up statues to Nell Gwynne and Lady Godiva, but never so far as I know to a copper.'

'There may perhaps,' said the Madam, eyeing him acidly, 'be yet *another* male profession that's not been commemorated by a statue.'

Frankie laughed: so generous a laugh that it put everyone at ease again. 'Oh, I grant you that!' he said. 'Just imagine it! A public monument to Pal Joey! Still,' he continued, 'that's how I feel. They say that coppers suppress crime. My own belief is they create it: they spread a criminal atmosphere where none existed. After all— look at it from their point of view. A soldier to succeed needs wars, whatever he may say to the contrary. In just the same way as a copper, to get on, needs crime.'

The Madam, who'd by now decided Frankie was a nuisance but on the whole a comparatively harmless one since his girl seemed to have him well in hand, said in a spirit of compromise, 'I'm prepared to allow you, Frankie, that the recent changes in the laws, so far as our business is concerned, have led to situations which make corruption very much more probable.'

'Yeah. But try telling the British public that!'

'I should not,' said the Madam with a faint smile, 'dream of doing anything of the kind.'

'Maybe not. But until the day when they wake up and find what's happened, the great British public will continue to believe in coppers. And shall I tell you why?'

Nobody wanted to hear, but their collective, unspoken female wisdom considered it simpler to let him get it off his chest than to try to interrupt him.

'In the first place,' said Frankie, 'it's *not* because the public as a whole respects the law, but merely because it's law-abiding, which is a very different matter.'

A bell rang, and the confidential maid departed.

'As a matter of fact they're not even so much law-abiding, as *respectable*: take away an Englishman's respectability, and you've taken his most cherished possession.'

The bisexual whore rose silently and also took her leave.

'Now, deep down we English, let me tell you, are a cruel and violent race. Yes, you may look at me like that, but cruel and violent is what we are. But at the same time we're respectable, like I've said, and have to live jam-packed on a microscopic island. So what do we do? We check our violence and cruelty by force: by our own force of will and by employing a force of witch-doctors or high-priests called coppers, who help us to restrain ourselves and who we worship for it.'

Frankie's girl shifted a bit uneasily; but the Madam remained calmly poised upon her Louis XXII chair.

'And what is more, just like the tribe does to the witch-doctor, we unload our guilty feelings on the coppers; the law, here in England, is the licensed keeper of our own bad conscience.'

There was a silence.

'And there's another aspect. Being cruel and violent, the Englishman knows he *might* commit a crime: a big one: headline stuff! Of course—he doesn't. But being at heart something of a criminal, he worships the man that he himself's set up to punish him if he did so.'

The Madam at last rose. 'I see, dear,' she said gently to the girl, 'your Frank's a very thoughtful boy. I hope for your sake his cock is even bigger than his brain.'

MR JUSTICE

THE habit of coppers of wishing or being ordered to 'hunt in pairs' has one great disadvantage to lone-wolves and philosophers in the Force. Long hours shared in isolation with one single other man will cause all but the most resolute or bone-headed to exchange confidences (which they should or would have preferred to have kept to themselves) with their momentary companion. So does the warder chat with the condemned prisoner, the isolated soldier with his erstwhile foe, or do the husband and wife who've already signed the deeds of separation if circumstances force them to be alone together.

The star sleuth sat with Edward in the bread-delivery van: and even his resilient spirit was cracking beneath the strain. He deeply resented, in the first place, that the Detective-sergeant had given him (him!) this flatfoot job to do. And as for Edward, if the boy had been really stupid as most of them were, or really inspired as he himself was, his company would have been at any rate tolerable. But Edward's mixture of brains and of professional ignorance and ineptitude (for so the star sleuth esteemed him) were nicely calculated to irritate an expert performer who had but recently himself fathomed many of the major mysteries of the copper's art.

'Another one going in,' said Edward, making an entry in his note-book.

'You can see in the dark?' asked the star sleuth.

'I've trained myself to write without a light,' said Edward.

'Well, you're wasting your time. *I* fill up my note-book *after* the event by use of my well-trained memory, and keep my brains cool for the event itself.'

'Maybe,' said Edward, who was growing sure enough of himself to resent the star sleuth's patronage quite a bit. 'But we've got to make certain your evidence and mine are going to tally.'

'Time enough for that. Though I might tell you one thing, youngster, that you *don't* know yet. They'll tell you the evidence of *two* officers will always nail a conviction. Well, in a magistrate's court that may be so but not, believe me, with a judge and jury—of which I don't think you've yet had a very vast experience.'

'Why?' Edward asked, vexed not to know.

'Here's why. Let's say you and I are on a case—see?—and we've both cross-checked our evidence. Right. When *I* go in to give mine, *you* have to stay outside. And when *you* come in to give yours I can stay in court but I can't speak to you, or alter what I've already said.'

'And so?'

'And so this. The defending counsel if he's got any brains, and most of them have or they wouldn't earn their huge fees, will ask me a-hundred-and-one questions about circumstances we just didn't think of—like was the prisoner wearing a cap or was it a hat?— and then when you come in, ask you the same questions and very probably get a rather different set of answers. This sows quite a bit of doubt in the jury's mind. I've often seen an acquittal got that way.'

'So what do we do?'

'That's it. One prosecuting witness is often better than two, even if uncorroborated. You can't contradict yourself, see: that is, provided you remember all you said if there's a re-examination.'

Edward Justice pondered. 'The courts are very tricky,' he said. 'In fact, I'm beginning to realize what goes on in them's a much bigger battle than all that takes place before you and the prisoner get there.'

'Ah! The light's dawning on you at last! My goodness! If only one young copper in a hundred realized what you've just said!'

Edward was silent.

'I'll tell you something,' said the star sleuth. 'Our real enemy isn't the criminals: it's the courts.'

'Our enemy?'

'Yes. Here's how I see it. *We are the law.* I say this because in the whole United Kingdom we're the only people who really *know*—and I mean *know*—what actually goes on. You admit that's so?'

'And then?'

'Well—picture this. The set-up in the Force we can manipulate, once we know how. And the criminals—well, as you know, there's a thousand and one ways of controlling them. Even in the courts, so long as it's only at the lawyer level, there are pressures that can be brought to bear. For instance: suppose you're a barrister who sometimes prosecutes, sometimes defends. If you win a lot of acquittals you're not likely to get a lot of prosecuting work to do, are you?'

'I suppose not, but . . .'

'Or take solicitors. Most of those the criminals use are living on criminal money themselves and often getting more of it than they should, in ways their professional bodies mightn't like to hear about. Now, they know this, they know we know it and pressures can be brought to bear.'

'Yes, I see that. But when . . .'

'All right, I'm coming to that. *But*, as I said at the outset, in the courts there's one thing we can't get at at all—except in a way that I'll explain to you: and that's the magistrates and judges—certainly, at any rate, the judges—and also to a certain extent the juries. Except—and mark my words—for this: we can get at all three by working on their ignorance, fear and vanity.'

'We can?'

'We can. As for ignorance, remember this. Judges used to be lawyers, and in their careers there's not much they haven't learned about by seeing it passing before them when they were working in the courts.'

'And so?'

'But *seeing* a thing is *not* the same as *living* it. When you go to a theatre you see the show: in fact it's put on for you, and you're in the best seats with the actors all facing you and smiling. But you're still not an actor, are you? You can see a thousand shows, and still know nothing about show-business whatever. Well, with the judges it's the same: they don't really *know*; and if they don't know you can blind them, if only to a limited extent.'

'But fear, you said. They're not afraid of us . . .'

'No? You'd think so, wouldn't you? The justices, here in England, are the top men in the land: way up above the generals and admirals and cabinet ministers, even. But—never forget—judges in history *have* been tried themselves. In fact, over on the Continent it's happened in our lifetime—very often, too. They're way up there, but they've got very far to fall! And if ever they *do*, who do you think will call round in the small hours to collect them?'

'Us?'

'Exactly. We, boy, you see, are even more permanent than they are and they know it. They're not fools, and because of this some-where deep down they fear us.'

'And their vanity? They're vain, you'd say?'

'Well—I ask you! What's the big, big bribe here in England? Come on—tell me! Is it money? Not a bit of it! Once you get above a certain level it's *honours*, man, and fancy-dress. You think I'm just being sarcastic? No, boy! To be dressed up in wigs and gowns and call himself lord and be surrounded by pomp and circumstance is worth *millions* to almost any Englishman. And judges—well, they love it! And if a man deep inside himself is vain, and what is worse —or better, from our point of view—*publicly* vain, then you can always play upon that weakness. "Yes, my lord. As you say, my lord." And, "As your lordship please." '

Edward reflected deeply, then said to the star sleuth, 'You don't think, then, that beyond us and beyond the courts and judges there's anything like an actual *justice* involved?'

'No.'

'It's all just personalities and procedure?'

'It's conventions: social customs, you might say. These change and alter, often radically, as anyone who's studied history a bit will know. But only one thing doesn't alter—and that's us: the men who *enforce* the laws, whatever they may be. And so I tell you: *we* are the courts, *we* are the judges, *we* are *justice!*' Edward, though highly excited by all this, was not sure by the soft, icy tone of his companion's voice whether he had a madman or a genius (or both) sitting beside him. Now the star sleuth's voice dropped to its normal mumble as he added, 'And even the stupid public and those fools in parliament, in their own way, admit this. Because according to the acts they've passed, if anyone shoots a lawyer—even a judge— and not for robbery, it isn't capital: but if a man kills one of us for any reason in the world, then—boy, he's hanged! This sets us up above the rest—above the lot of them, top men and all! Our lives are protected by the hangman's rope!'

Edward said deferentially but with considerable reserve (as one does when making a remark to anyone which one both wants him to believe and also be able to say, afterwards, one did not mean), 'So according to you, you should make a suspect feel that we, "the law", *are* the law.'

'Yes.'

Then Edward said, 'That's not how the Detective-sergeant sees it, I imagine.'

'I don't suppose so. That pensionable clot!'

'They don't serve their purpose then, according to you, his type?'

'Yes—for all sorts of things that don't really matter. Like clearing the public off the streets as they did so well when old Tito came here, or marshalling crowds when they indulge in political demonstrations, or for horseback parades in Hyde Park when we're drawn up just as if we were *soldiers*! for a royal inspection. For all that, yes. But for the real work: well—what do *you* think?'

'I quite like the old boy,' Edward said.

'I'm not talking about *liking*. Do you respect him?'

Edward didn't answer.

'You've got to make up your mind,' the star sleuth said, 'right from the outset which kind of copper you're going to be: a robot or a man with *power*.'

After a short pause Edward said, 'As a matter of fact, I've found the Detective-sergeant helpful to me.'

'Yeah? Well, I see nothing against that . . .'

'No. He's put me on guard against one or two little things he's mentioned.'

'He has? Such as what? Do you mean that I found out about your girl?'

'So it was you.'

'No secret about it, matey. I'm bound to investigate you a bit, aren't I, if you join our little lot and I'm going to have to put my own life and professional career to a certain extent into your two clumsy hands . . .'

'But did you have to tell anyone?'

'I didn't: nothing reported, I mean. I just *mentioned* it.'

'I don't see the difference.'

'You don't? There's a *lot* of difference, as you'll grow to learn.'

'Is there? Well, here's something for you to learn please, too. I resent your interfering with my private life, and I'll ask you here and now to stop it.'

'Oh! So I'm being threatened! Well! Listen to me, boy, I'm not in the habit of giving advice because it's a thing much too precious to give away and anyhow, the kind of person who *needs* advice never knows how to *use* it if you give it to him. But I will tell you this, and it's entirely for your own good because personally I just don't care a fuck. Drop that girl. Look at it any way you like, if you want to get on—in fact if you want to stay with us at all—well, boy, it's your only logical solution.'

MR JUSTICE (STILL)

LOOKING out of the institutional window (too tall for its width) of his nominal residence at the section-house, Edward was mildly alarmed to see his girl standing on the pavement opposite. Since no message had come up to him that anyone wanted to see him and it was scarcely probable that he'd happened to look out at the precise moment she'd arrived, he was even more alarmed. For she certainly didn't know as well as he did that the most conspicuous possible thing to do, in England, particulary for a woman, is to wait in a public street: even if she'd waited on the anonymous benches of the station itself she'd have attracted far less attention. He hurried down.

Out in the street he saw her some way off, which partly re-assured him. And catching up with her he learned with approval but anxiety that she'd kept walking round the block until he'd appeared, and that a matter of some urgency—two, in fact—had brought her out of hiding. The first was that she was pregnant; the second, that someone—nobody yet knew who—had visited her father's house during his absence in peculiar circumstances.

Though she told him the first of these two things last, he genuinely

considered it to be in every way the more important. For one reason
because it clearly brought—in some way or another—his relationship with his girl to a state of crisis; but even more because this
news excited and delighted Edward unexpectedly. Although in
their discussions of this possibility they'd both agreed it was for the
present highly undesirable, and had taken steps in a rather hap-
hazard way to guard against the danger, Edward had always feared,
in secret, that he was somehow incapable of paternity: just as he
had not been sure until he'd first loved his girl in that complete and
intimate way that he could actually *do* so, it needed the proof
positive that she now gave to him that he could without any doubt
become a father. Not that he had for the new life in her womb—or
for what it might become—as yet any feeling, fatherly or otherwise.
What he *did* feel was that his love for her—the total horizon of his
whole emotional life—was now—in spite of the manifold complications—entire and wonderful.

'So what shall we do?' she said.

'Let's pop in here for a tea and a sit-down.'

Side by side, and Ted filled with an immense sense of *possession*,
they discussed their predicament in quiet voices. 'I suppose you
don't want to say it, Edward,' she said, 'but I *could* do away
with it.'

'No!'

'Why? Because it's illegal?' And she smiled rather wryly.

'No: because it's too dangerous to you.'

'It's not really . . . Not all *that* dangerous . . .'

'You sure of that?'

'I think so.'

'No! We can't risk anything happening to you.'

'Very well, then. What?'

'You'll have to have it in the normal way.'

'But, Edward. As things are, it won't be exactly normal.'

'You mean us not being wed?'

'Yes.'

'Yes, I know. We must get the position straightened out. That's
what I meant to tell you when I came out to you this evening.'

'Why?'

'They've found out about us.'

'Who?'

'Several: it's not officially known to the Force, but there's individuals who know.'

The girl looked at him and said, 'So you won't have to pretend any longer, Edward, that I don't exist.'

'No. They know.'

'I see. So what do we do?'

Edward stared into space, then said, 'If it's you or the Force, I choose you. I can always earn my living some other way, I'm competent, you know, believe me. But I've been thinking a lot, and there may be a way out.'

She looked at him harder.

'If your Dad emigrated.'

'Emigrated? Dad? Why should he?'

'If he sees it's to your advantage and to his own to make a new start, and if I make it worth his while.'

'But Edward: how can you?'

'I think I can. He must have a bit saved of his own, and I believe I can make up the single fare and enough over, given a bit of time.'

'But what difference will it make if Dad should go?'

'I've been looking into precedents: I mean of marriages with girls of—well, of dubious parentage—and it's been okay in several cases if the parents are dead, of course, or gone away for good.'

'You sure?'

'I think they'd wear it—but only if he's right out of the country: Canada or Australia—somewhere like that.'

'I see.'

'But there is one other aspect. Suppose he refused to go. I may have to ask you if you don't mind if I put pressure on him.'

'Pressure? How?'

'Make him believe we're going to get something on him.'

The girl said, 'Oh, Edward! And he's stayed in the clear so long!'

'So he says, I know. But what can we do?'

'And this money, Ted. It's a bit of a race against time, isn't it? I mean you've not got all that many months to get it, and get permission to marry, before I have the baby.'

'I've thought of that: and it's why I'll have to get it quick.'

'I still think you won't shift Dad. Him leave Kensal Green? And take money from you?'

'Well, as a matter of fact he already has done.'

'Dad has? Taken money?'

'Yes. Only to look after it, though. I've already made a bit, you see, and the best person I could think of to look after it for us—I mean the only *reliable* person—was your father.'

'And he agreed?'

'Oh, yes . . . So we've already discussed financial matters.'

'You didn't tell me, Ted.'

'No, dear. I thought it best not. Well: what you say?'

The girl stirred her empty cup. 'For me,' she said, 'it's like this. I want you, Ted, in the best way I can keep you, whatever that turns out to be—but there are limits. I don't mind so much what arrangements you have to make with Dad, but I want you to promise me if he refused to go, and you let me *have* my baby, then you'll marry me even if it means leaving the Force.'

'Okay,' said Edward. 'That's a promise. Though if he *does* refuse to go and I can't make him, I will ask you, all the same, to let me check up on the abortion aspects.'

'What do you mean?'

'Well, dear, I know it's a big sacrifice, but you've made me think and I'd like to have a word with the station doctor—very indirect, of course—about the actual danger. Because if I can't shake your Dad at once and it's only a question of the time it takes to persuade him, it's be a pity to leave the Force if we did manage to persuade him later on.'

'Yes, I see.'

Edward looked at her. 'You mean you don't want an abortion—not in any circumstances?'

'I haven't quite said that . . .'

'And you're not prepared to have the baby out of wedlock . . .'

'No, Ted. That I don't want: if I have him, I want to have him legitimate.'

'All right: I think I've got it. Thank you, dear, for being so reasonable about it all. Now, then. What about this man you said visited your Dad's place?'

'According to Dad, Ted, he's certain someone's been in the house, but there's no sign of breaking and entering or anything at all.'

'Yeah. I think I know who it might be. Your Dad didn't find anything *left* in the place? Nothing compromising, I mean?'

'He didn't say so . . .'

'And nothing missing?'

'He didn't say that either . . . But who do you think it might be, Ted? A thief?'

'No, a copper. Colleague of mine who doesn't like me.'

'But why should he try to harm Dad?'

'To try to harm me. I'll tell you who it is—in confidence—it's one of our vice boys I'm on a job with at the moment—very clever feller and very dangerous—who's got a down on me.'

'But why?'

'I really and truly don't know: but these things do happen in the Force. I'll speak to your Dad about that as well, and put him on his guard. Meantime, I think there's something *you* could do to help.'

'Me? How?'

Edward smiled at her. 'If I pointed out this feller to you, do you think you might consider trying to play up to him a bit?'

'How? You mean flirt with him, or so?'

'Yes. Nothing more than that . . . But it might help to find a way to get something on him, too, to keep him quiet.'

'Well, I'm not sure, Edward. If you think it's wise . . . But I'm not very glamorous, you know . . .'

'Nor's he. Anyway, we'll see. I'll keep you well in the picture, dear. Glory! What a morning! I'm glad all that's tidied up just now.'

He made to get up, but the girl detained him. 'There is just one other thing,' she said.

'No! Well, in for a penny . . .'

'Listen, Edward. You remember that couple we saw at the wrestling that night, and you commented on, who came to settle in the same block as we do . . .'

'Yeah . . . Whore and her ponce, I'd say. But not my area and not my business—we don't want trouble near the flat . . .'

'No, I know that. But the woman, Ted, the prostitute. She *knows* about us.'

'Knows? How can she know? What makes you think so? Anything she's said?'

'Nothing she's said, but the way she *looks* at me.'

'*Looks* at you! Oh, come off it, darling. What is this: feminine intuition?'

'Edward, she knows *something*: I'm convinced of it.'

'That we're not married, maybe.'

'Something more. The other day a uniformed officer passed by just as I passed *her*, and she looked at *him* and then she looked at me, and she smiled.'

'She smiled!'

'Yes.'

'I'll give her something to smile for . . . And the ponce? Any angles there?'

'No, I've scarcely seen him. He's very discreet.'

'He'd better be. Look, darling, I'll investigate that a bit as well, but now I really must get off down to the station. Thank you for all your loyalty, and thank you for being the most wonderful girl any man ever had and I know I don't deserve it.'

They kissed quietly, the girl very silent, and then went out of the café separately. At the station, the Detective-sergeant called Edward in and said to him, 'Lad, there's been a development.'

'In this Madam case, sir?'

'Yes. What d'you know? She's phoned us.'

'Well, she's got a sauce, sir. What was her reason?'

'There's been a theft—quite a big one, she says. From one of her clients, I dare say, though she didn't say so.'

'And you want me to go down, sir?'

'Yes. Find out all you can, of course, but be very careful *not* to give the impression we've got other ideas about her. She hasn't seen you, has she?'

'Not so far as I know, sir . . . But isn't she taking a chance calling us in like this?'

'Well, *she* evidently doesn't think so . . . Remember, as she sees it her set-up in that place is foolproof. No, her real danger as she probably weighs it up is that the client who's been robbed—if I'm right about that—is more of a danger just at present than we or any-one else are.'

'But sir: she must know *we* know what she's up to.'

'Oh, of course she does! There's no need to hide that fact when you see her—just give her no hint that we're planning a little party for her.'

Edward got up. 'Well, sir, all I can say is I wish I had her nerve.'

The Detective-sergeant smiled, then looked very cautious and said, 'It's just possible between you and me, constable, there may be another angle: and that's why I want you to tread very warily.'

'Sir?'

'It *is* just possible she's subbing somebody—somebody in the Force, I mean—and getting protection. I don't *know* this, mind you —I have to make a few discreet enquiries—but it is a possibility. If that were happening it would, of course, give her extra confidence and we'd have to find out exactly what the situation is—inter-departmentally, I mean—before we actually stage the raid we have in mind.'

'Yes, sir. May I make a suggestion?' The Detective-sergeant nod-ded. 'It might be, sir, that someone who's got no authority—I mean no real *position*—is taking something from her and making her believe she's got real protection when she hasn't.'

The officer smiled. 'Bright boy,' he said. 'Yes, that's another one that had occurred to me. Any ideas who it might be, if it is?'

'No, sir. Not yet, anyway . . .'

'Well, son, keep me posted. I may be the brains, but you're my eyes and ears, remember. So get out now and use them for me.'

Calling at the front door of the Madam's brothel was, for Edward, a strange experience resembling, perhaps, that of a love-lorn gas-inspector who, contemplating in vain from its exterior for so long the house of his adored one, suddenly finds he's ordered round there on routine business to check the meter. The confidential maid admit-ted him, and he was soon in the presence of the Madam.

It was instantly apparent that she possessed to handle Edward an enormous asset that neither of them, before meeting, could possibly have predicted. This was that the Madam was a 'motherly' person (in spite of being childless and of having had, ages ago, her ovaries removed) who could soothe the profound solitude that lay at the very centre of Edward's personality, and was the chief cause of his happiness in the Force and of his deep attachment to his girl. But this pit of loneliness was bottomless; and only time or even death would really fill it. Meanwhile, anyone who could restore to Edward something of his sense of self was certain of some measure of his gratitude.

This the old Madam, no mean empirical psychologist, spotted instantly as she sat Edward down on the chintz sofa, perched herself on a chair before him, and laid all her troubles eagerly and confidingly in his broad lap. She kept, she said, as he must know, residential chambers patronized by the very nicest kind of gent. (As a matter of fact she *did* have several curious, permanent tenants in the house in rooms unsuitable, for various reasons, for other purposes, and who she felt lent tone—if not legality—to the premises as a whole.) Very well, then. One of these gentlemen—she was most reluctant to divulge his name, but she could say he was a luminary in the legal profession—had very foolishly (as even luminaries sometimes are) brought a young woman to his apartment, and after this young woman's departure he'd noticed that a snuff-box—for the legal gentleman was addicted to this charming and old-world (or camp and disgusting) habit of taking the stuff—which was not only an heirloom of great sentimental value but also, according to the legal gent, insured for £350, had gone; and if it were not rapidly recovered he'd be forced to make the whole thing public as otherwise the insurance company wouldn't consider a claim. 'I know,' the Madam now concluded, 'that *your* only thought, officer, as the good detective I'm sure you are, is to catch the thief. But *my* chief preoccupation is to get back the snuff-box for my tenant and avoid, if possible, my house getting publicity and an undesirable bad name.'

Edward, both by interest in the Madam and by professional decorum, had said nothing yet. As she appeared to have finished (always let women *finish*, he'd discovered: there's nothing they like better than for you to interrupt them), he said to her, 'Who do you suspect? The girl?'

The Madam blinked her eyes and said, 'It must be her. Who else could it be?'

'This girl been here before?'

'Well, yes, as a matter of fact, yes, she has on one or two occasions. And I've always thought her—the little I've seen of her, of course, for I don't interfere with my tenant's private affairs though I do, naturally, keep an eye on things—a very attractive and well-spoken young lady. But there is one other thing about her.'

The Madam paused and Edward, eyeing her coolly, still said nothing.

'I happen to know,' the Madam said, 'she has a boy friend who I think she calls Frankie who I *don't* think is a very desirable sort of young man at all. I did see them once together, as it happens, and I wasn't favourably impressed by him. I'm not saying, mind you, that he did it or even that he egged her on. But I *do* know he's an undesirable influence and I have, of course, told my tenant that the girl is not to visit my house again under any circumstances whatever.'

'I may need,' said Edward, 'to talk to your tenant. But meanwhile you'd better give me the girl's address.'

The Madam instantly gave it. Edward looked at it, remained impassive, then looked at her. 'May I ask you, madam,' he said, 'how you happen to have this girl's address at your finger-tips?'

A shaft of venom came into the Madam's eyes as they fluttered, and she said, 'My tenant told me it.'

'How did *he* know?'

'*That*, I couldn't say.'

'I see. And when you saw her with this friend of hers, where was it?'

'I don't see . . .

'Where was it?'

'In the street.'

'Not here?'

'Certainly not!'

'And not at the address you've given me?'

'Of course not! I don't even know where it is—except, of course, that it's somewhere up in Kilburn.'

'Very well,' said Edward, rising. 'Thank you very much.'

The Madam came closer, looked up at him like a corrupt innocent in a Rossetti painting, and putting one ringed hand on his vigorous arm said, 'I *do* hope, officer, you can recover this jewel for me with the minimum of fuss.'

'I'll do my best.'

She lowered her eyes, then said, 'My tenant—confidentially, of course—would be willing to offer a quite considerable reward if it

were returned to him without any publicity. I don't know how much
—he hasn't said—but certainly at least half of its full value.'

'I'll remember that,' said Edward.

MR LOVE AND MR JUSTICE

FRANKIE was sitting drinking lager and lime with the star ponce,
and his girl was sulking in the adjacent bedroom. She was sulking,
in the first place, because she didn't approve of Frankie's friend
being there at all. In earlier days he'd never have taken a silly
chance like that (hadn't she always told him—business and pleasure
must be kept quite separate?) and now, really, he was getting care-
less (the number one—short of impotence—defect in any ponce).

But the chief and most vital source of argument had been about
her miscarriage. In spite of precautions unwanted pregnancies, in a
prostitute's life, can occur as they can in anybody's (if only, she
thought, the Americans or the Russians or whoever it was would
hurry up and perfect those magic pills you popped into your mouth)
and Frankie's girl, in the past, had always taken these mishaps in
her stride, seen her favourite doctor (up in Tufnell Park), rested up
afterwards and gone back to work again. This, without telling
Frankie, she had recently done once more and he, when she told
him, had exploded in a rage! Would the child have been his, he'd
asked? Well—almost certainly: at any rate, very likely. Then didn't
she realize, the stupid bitch, he wanted her to have his son if nature
sent him? Why the hell hadn't she *consulted* him about it?

Now, in the first place, it'd honestly never occurred to her that he
might feel like this; and in the second—well, both as a woman and
as a prostitute wasn't it *her* affair? Why! the man was beginning to
behave to her like a *husband*! And to make matters worse, because
of her resting there was no ready money—and Frankie, if you
please, 'didn't like to' touch their *savings*! Well! What in the hell are
savings for? So she brooded in the bedroom, doing her nails nine-
teen times each and wondering if she should sink her dignity and go
in and look at the telly. Masculine laughter, coming from the adjoin-
ing room, added mightily to her exasperation.

Looking up (as we do when the palaeolithic man inside us tele-graphs his warning), she saw something that roused all her pro-fessional alertness and—like a ship's officer who, in a storm, may instantly forget a quarrel or postpone it—she hastened to the room next door. 'Frankie,' she cried. 'You remember that couple at the wrestling?'

'Eh? Yeah.'

'Well—*he's* coming over.'

'Who is it?' said the star ponce, whose reflexes were also racing at a calm and well-oiled tempo.

'A copper,' Frankie said, '—or I believe so. He's shacked up with a girl here—something shady, I don't know what—and he's never given us any kind of trouble . . .'

'Well, he's coming over,' said the girl.

'You want to go?' said Frankie to his friend.

'Why should I—if you don't want me to?'

'Thanks, pal. I may possibly need a witness. Baby, as for you, you'd better get back in that bedroom.'

The girl made as if to speak and then retired—but grabbing, on her way, a large pile of Yank mags. The two men took another tranquil drink, nerves tingling, waiting for that big event in the ponce's life—the *knock*.

It came.

Frankie got up, opened the front door, and closed it behind him so that he faced Edward on the balcony. He said nothing at all and looked at Edward, relaxed and not particularly hostile, in the eyes.

'I expect you know who I am,' said Edward.

'Sure. It's written all over you,' Frankie said.

Edward smiled slightly and said, 'Could I come in?'

'You're *asking* to?' said Frankie.

'Certainly. It's an enquiry . . . I haven't got a warrant or anything like that . . .'

'I didn't suppose you had or you wouldn't have asked me, and you wouldn't have been alone.'

'Well. Can I come in?'

'I don't see why not.'

Frankie opened the door, invited Edward to sit down but did not

offer him a drink or, for that matter, introduce him to the star ponce
—who throughout the interview did not look at Edward (or be seen
to) any more than Edward did (or seemed to do) at him.

'I'll come straight to the point,' Edward said. 'It's about a theft.
You may know nothing whatever about it, and I may be disturbing
you for nothing, in which case, of course, I apologize. But on the
other hand if you could help me at all over it, I think it might be to
your advantage.'

'So far,' said Frankie, 'you haven't said a thing I understand.'

'No. Well, to make it brief. Can I be frank?'

'If any copper ever was . . .'

Edward smiled. 'Well, put it like this. The young lady you live
with has been in business, I believe, up till quite recently at a
certain premises. Do I make myself clear?'

'Go on . . .'

'Well, now. It's been reported to me that at these premises there's
been a theft.'

'Yeah? Of what?'

'A snuff-box.'

'A what?'

'A jewelled snuff-box of a certain value which we—and the person
who's lost it, naturally—are anxious to recover.'

'I suppose they would be.'

'Yes. Well—that's all I have to tell you.'

The two men looked at each other. And their looks had one thing
in common (which is a very rare one among coppers and among
ponces, and even among any men at all) which was that neither
feared the other in the least.

Edward got up. 'I expect you know,' he said, 'where you can find
me if there's anything that you can tell me soon. But it would have
to be soon, please, because if I can't settle this thing one way then
I'll be obliged, you see, to settle it another.'

'Yes,' Frankie said, rising too. 'I know where I can find you. You
live over there, don't you, with a young woman?'

Edward nodded.

'I didn't know,' said Frankie, 'that in the Force they allowed you
that particular kind of freedom.'

'Well,' Edward said beside the door, 'I dare say, whatever

profession or activity you may have, you never find that you're entirely free in it.'

He smiled slightly and Frankie let him out. Then cutting short the star ponce (who had accumulated a wealth of professional diagnosis of the situation that he was positively bursting his handsome body to impart), Frankie went into the bedroom, closed the door behind him, pulled his girl to her feet and said, 'Have you been stealing?'

'Stealing, Frankie?'

Frankie slapped her face. She slapped back. Frankie slapped her really hard and she fell down on the bed. Outside, the star ponce slightly smiled: the familiarity of the episode was reassuring.

The girl looked up at him and said, 'Frankie, that's the first time you've hit me.'

'It's not.'

'It's the first time you've hit me like *that*.'

'Well, I want an answer. Did you knock off a snuff-box at the Madam's?'

The girl looked incredulous, then furious, then laughing a bit hysterically she rummaged among her lingerie and cried, 'You mean *this*?'

'Yeah. Why you pinch it?'

'*Pinch* it? Are you crazy? The old bastard *gave* it to me.'

'You lying?'

'Oh, go and get stuffed, Frank! You're needling me too much!'

'He gave it to you, you say?'

'Of course he fucking gave it to me! He was high as a kite at the time and now I suppose he's saying I took it from him in his drunken stupor. Well—what should I have done? Got his permission in writing? He kept tucking it inside my bra and saying, "*Chérie*, this is for you," and crap like that.'

Frankie held the box, looked at her and said, 'I'm sorry, baby. But you should have told me.'

'What was there to tell? I've had presents before, often enough—dozens of them, I've had.'

'Things like this?'

'Why? Is it all that valuable?'

'That's what the copper was here about—I suppose you heard.'

'No. I tried to listen, but he spoke too low.'

Frankie considered, put the box in his pocket and said, 'Look, baby. I want you to go out and take a little walk.'

'Why?'

'Because I say so. Just for an hour or so.'

'You want to talk it over with your pal?'

'Yeah.'

'I'm too stupid to give an opinion, I suppose?'

'Just do as I say, baby, there's a honey.'

The girl agreed, not because she thought Frankie was right but because she knew the convention of male sagacity in crises— particularly those closely related to the law—was a powerful one in 'the game'; and come to that, it was the boys themselves who so often *were* in greater danger.

'Okey-doke,' she said. 'You win.'

When she'd gone, the two men embarked on their analysis of the angles. 'As I see it,' said the star ponce as a Queen's counsel might to a promising junior, 'it's quite clear the copper wants the box and not your girl. I'd also say he's called here on his own initiative. Reasons: he came alone and he was very nice, which coppers never do or are if they mean business.'

'He wants the box for himself, you think?'

'No: there's probably a reward attached. Well, if you can square it with your girl I'd say the simplest is to give it to him *but*, if you take my tip, you'll do it in front of two witnesses—outside the game, if possible—*and* if possible, invisible to him.'

'I'm certain,' said Frankie, 'he's up to something with that girl of his he doesn't want generally known. So I don't think he's likely to pursue the matter very far, knowing I might bring *that* up. I'd better try to find out exactly what his set-up with the woman is.'

'If he gets awkward at all,' said the star ponce, 'you might try to implicate her. Lay her, I mean.'

'Boy, have you *seen* her?'

'No. But all women are much the same from the navel down. There are, of course,' the star ponce continued, 'other aspects. You could consider, through your own woman, trying to have a go at him—I mean some compromising situation with witnesses and perhaps a camera.'

'Yeah.'

'Or,' the star ponce went on, warming to his work, 'there's possibly this other angle. I couldn't help hearing you and your girl having a bit of an argument.'

'No?'

'No. Now, I don't know . . . I don't know how you're fixed and I'm not trying at all to interfere. But if it *did* happen you wanted to cut out from the lass and latch on with another—and believe me, Frankie, there's plenty of them who'd not say no—this would certainly be the opportunity.'

'You mean,' said Frankie smiling slightly, 'I could just disappear and let the law take its course?'

'That's it! It's not you, after all, who's committed any theft . . . supposing, that is, she's wrong about what she said to you and it *was* one—and at any rate it *looks* like one to some people, doesn't it. Well, you could fix things in that way: just leave her and the copper to sort the matter out.'

Frankie got up. 'No, I don't think so, boy,' he said. 'I'm not tied to that chick—don't think that—I'm not tied to *any* woman and I never will be. But I'd certainly never shop her, and that's what your suggestion would amount to.'

'If you say so. What I was doing, Francis, was considering all the angles and the aspects.'

'Oh, I'm very grateful, man—don't misunderstand me.'

The star ponce rose too. 'So what you going to do—I mean with the box?' he said.

Frankie took it out of his pocket and threw it a foot in the air. 'Hang on to it a while and see. Perhaps I'll do a little investigation on my own account just like a copper. Perhaps there might even be a little bit of rough stuff, too, like they do from time to time.'

MR LOVE

In the next days Frankie took the following precautions.

He visited the Stepney Bengali, told him to draw three hundred pounds for him, bought a single air ticket to Monrovia and checked the validities in his passport.

He had a long conversation with the janitor at the Kilburn flat—who, he'd long discovered, had formerly seen harpooning service upon whalers—made him within the privacy of his quarters at the lodge a comradely gift (for old times' sake), and suggested it was undesirable to have among them in the block a copper in disguise who'd probably get busted anyway for living with a woman out of wedlock, and that if this copper's flat by any chance should become vacant somehow, he, Frankie, knew someone who'd be very glad to offer double—maybe more—the usual key-money that he, the janitor, expected.

He then followed Edward's girl one morning she went out shopping and, choosing his moment in an empty street came up suddenly beside her, immediately said, 'Give your copper boy friend this,' dropped a little package in her shopping-bag, and made off at a steady pace before she could reply.

To round matters off he sent this anonymous telegram, by telephone from a call-box, to the local station of the Force: WHERE DOES EDWARD JUSTICE LIVE AND WHY.

Finally, to clear the decks for any possible action he sent his girl to spend a short holiday with her faith-healing Mum at Walthamstow. She departed reluctantly under protest, and in the taxi said to him, 'Frankie, you ever thought of getting married?'

'We've discussed that. No.'

'I mean know. The way things are, and now you've saved up a bit.'

Frankie looked at her. 'Are you trying to tell me, babe,' he said, 'you'd consider giving up the game if we got wed?'

'Yeah. As a matter of fact that's it.'

'Well! That's rather sweet of you! But honest, baby, I'm not the marrying kind.'

'No, I suppose not. But think it over, will you, when this thing blows over? We could move up north somewhere, one of the ports, and open up a caff or club or something for the seamen.'

'And the girls!'

'Well, why not! For the both of them. But on the up-and-up—legitimate.'

He kissed her. 'I'll think about it, dear,' he said.

She reached forward, pulled aside the driver's window and yelled at his neck, 'Not that way—that way!' then took Frankie's arm again and said, 'I wish you'd let me handle all this for you, dear.'

'And what would you do?'

'Me? Use my fanny for you. I mean, find out why they're getting at you, and who, and offer him the best time of his life.'

'Thanks, dear—but no good. A copper wouldn't know a really good time if he had it.'

MR JUSTICE

EDWARD was closeted with his girl's disreputable father: who as Edward's affairs had grown in their complexity had become, in a sense, increasingly his own. For the older man this new relationship was possible because Edward now stood revealed in spite of his hateful uniform as a creature, like himself, of common clay. Not that the father ever forgot Edward's status: in spite of their growing intimacy Edward, for him, was still more a copper than a son-in-law-to-be.

Amid the confusion of the father's workroom with its radios and tellies and cameras and miscellaneous junk, Edward unfolded all the plots and counter-plots by which he was now surrounded. One matter, at any rate, was satisfactorily disposed of—or almost so—between them: the father was willing to go abroad. A sufferer from lumbago, he believed the heat of the Central African Federation would benefit his condition; and in a land where brains and technical skill were needed (and manual labour which was painful to him would be available in plenty), he thought that he would find his niche. But what, Edward countered, about the immigration regulations? Wouldn't they check up on his past career?

To overcome this obstacle the older man had imagined a truly Napoleonic solution which he now disclosed to Edward with a crafty smile. He'd not applied for a resident permit but for one for visitors, and had already been sent the appropriate application forms. To Question 18, which asked, candidly, 'Have you ever been in prison?' he had simply and boldly written, 'No': relying on the magic that a completed form held in itself to those who had devised it and who, he imagined, would be most unlikely to check up; anyway, his 'trouble' had been a long while ago, and if *they* said 'No,' well, all right, he'd try somewhere else climatically suitable. If the visa was granted he would go there, look around, establish contacts and, he was certain, make himself useful enough for them to want to keep him in the Federation on a permanent basis. It was really after all, he added, only *political* undesirables they were anxious to exclude from the Rhodesias.

Edward on his side disclosed the business of the snuff-box, and the hopeful prospects its probable recovery held out of supplementing the nest-egg of the prospective emigrant. Edward did not consider it likely that Frankie, given time to meditate, would refuse to yield it up; and if he did prove obstinate, that situation could be faced as it arose. To bring pressure on the ponce he had, after reflection, hit on this: he'd called up Frankie's girl from a public-box (on the number kindly supplied, for a consideration, by the flat janitor—a good friend of his and a special constable, as well as an ex-seaman on a whaler) and the moment the receiver had been raised, had said immediately, 'Miss, this is a well-wisher in the Force to say if Frankie does as he's asked I promise there'll be no further trouble,' hanging up instantly without waiting for a reply.

'So that leaves us,' Edward said, 'with one vital thing outstanding: this visit you had, and who I've told you I think is at the bottom of it.'

The ex-criminal reflected. 'What I don't fathom yet,' he said, 'is this. If as you say it's a pal of yours in the Force who's trying to harm you by framing me—and from what I know of you and your pals the thing, in itself, is very possible—why doesn't he try to plant something on *you* direct? And if he chooses me, why does he come here and not plant anything at all?'

'Look,' Edward answered. 'I love your girl: now, you believe that, don't you? whatever you think about me and about the Force. Well, this man he's a clever one. He knows if he can get at you and so get at *her*, he gets at me worse than any other way. Also, he knows I'm on my guard and naturally I'd recognize him if he came snooping around my place at all.'

'Then why did he just come snooping around mine here and nothing else? Not plant anything, if that's what you think he's up to?'

'Well, it's a way we have: perhaps I shouldn't tell you, but it's this: always reconnoitre, if you can, before you act. It's laid down in all the manuals.'

'Is it? Oh, I see.'

'Besides, he may not have had the right *thing* to plant on you until he saw the situation here: I mean, what sort of item might seem credible.'

Edward realized his girl's father was looking very hard at him indeed. 'So you *do* plant things, you bastards,' the father said.

Edward paused, then answered, 'Look: do we have to go into all that again?'

'Sonny boy!' the father said, 'let me tell you something. I'm so glad I'm not you: that's all. You've all got minds like mazes: trick upon trick until you tie yourself in knots. Take care you don't get lost inside your own maze, boy, some day!'

Edward waited patiently for the father's natural resentment to subside (coppers are used to this—as used as doctors are to pain), then said, 'Now the thing is, he may come again. And if he does, this time I want to catch him water-tight, report him to my Detective-sergeant and get him busted, or anyway transferred. My Detective-sergeant doesn't like him, you see, and *none* of us likes a man who shops his comrades.'

Now, the father waited silently.

'So here's what I suggest. He'll very probably come here again soon and if he does, this time he'll have something with him. So we've got to catch him in the act. You follow me?'

'Yeah. I'm listening.'

'Now, I want to ask my girl—your girl—to come back and stay here with you for a while.'

'Why? You were anxious enough to get her away from me a time ago . . .'

'I know. But I want her out of the flat up there until I get things straightened out with this ponce I mentioned and also—this is the point and hear me out carefully please, don't raise your voice or be hasty—I want her here *when* this so-called star-sleuth colleague of mine shows up on the premises.'

'Why?'

'To fix him.'

'How?'

Edward looked round the room. 'Now, you've got cameras,' he said, 'and flashes. I want you to lock all the rooms every night except where my girl will be sleeping. And I want you, if possible, to snap the pair of them together.'

'Together doing what?'

'Nothing! What you take me for?'

'Well, what you take *me* for?'

'I said—don't be hasty! As soon as he's in the house I'll tell her she's to run out to him, even if he doesn't come into her room at all: you know—dishevelled and distressed and so on: she'll do it all right for me.'

The father looked at Edward and shook his head. 'And that's who my daughter wants to marry,' he said simply. 'Well, I give up! And how do we know he's in the house at all? I didn't last time . . .'

'But you were out. And you weren't expecting him. Look! He's not a magician, he can only get in through the doors or windows . . . You've not got a skylight?'

'No.'

'Well, I want you to wire them all: the ones he can get in at, anyway. Can you do that?'

'I could do . . .'

'Something silent: a light comes on in your room—or a faint buzz —then you grab your camera and go into action.'

'I see. So I go to bed with my camera every night for weeks?'

'No: a week should be enough. Then the case that we're both working on is over—anyway, the raid we're planning will be—and he'll probably lay off me after that. It's because we're together on this job that he's so riled and jealous. Once it's over I'll just warn him off, and tell him I know what he's been up to.'

'Why don't you do that now?'

'Because I want to compromise him if I can: I mean, turn the tables on him so that he'll never try anything again! Show him who I am and who he is!'

The father looked at Edward with faint pity. 'You think the photo you speak of, if I took it, would do that? Do they believe photos at all, then, in your Force?'

'I won't even have to show it to them: only to him and say I've got the negative.'

'And you think he's all that dangerous to you?'

'He and my Detective-sergeant are the only colleagues, so far as I can tell, that know about me and my girl. I think the Detective-sergeant's okay—I think he likes me; and if I can shut the other one up, by the time we've got you away we can put in the application properly and get married.'

'When you've got rid of me.'

'Don't be like that! You know your girl loves me and I do her and this is the only way I can see to fix it!'

The father put his hand in quite a friendly way on Edward's arm. 'You know,' he mildly said, 'you really are a nasty piece of work—a proper little scheming bastard. Also, I think you're over-wrought and what you're asking me to do's a lot of nonsense. Why don't you take a holiday for a while?'

'My leave's not due yet—and I need it for the honeymoon.'

'Yes. That's the funny thing—she loves you. She really does: Eve alone knows why. Well, I'll see what I can do. But I want you to understand there's to be no funny business with my girl inside my house, and the only *promise* I'm making you is that if you raise the balance of the funds, I'll go.'

The front bell rang and both men stiffened, as if it were already the star sleuth on the doorstep. But it was the girl: manifestly upset, and bursting with fell tidings.

Getting her story wrong-way-round chronologically (though right way in point of urgency), she began by crying out. 'It's disappeared!' Calm and adroit questioning by Edward extracted the story of Frankie's alarming deposition of the snuff-box in her shopping-bag, how she'd got home, found out what it was, put it away safely until Edward should arrive, but that now it had gone from where she'd placed it.

'And where was that?'

'Among my lingerie.'

'And why did you go out again?'

'Just to the pictures.'

'For how long?'

'As long as the big film.'

'It *must* be him!' Edward concluded. 'Well! Now we know what he's going to try and plant here.'

'Must be who?' asked the girl.

But the men ignored her. 'It couldn't,' the father said, 'be that ponce himself who's changed his mind and got it back . . . ?'

'Listen! The man's not crazy!'

'But if it's your colleague wasn't it enough, if he wanted to compromise you, to find it in your flat?'

'No. No, because he knew I could say I had it there ready to turn it in. But if it's found *here*, then it looks black for me—*and* for you: don't forget that!'

'I hadn't,' the father said. 'But there's one more thing. Couldn't it be he'll just take it to the Madam and get the reward instead of you?'

'How does he know she's offered one?'

'Well—he might know.'

'No, I don't think so,' Edward said emphatically, sure of his diagnosis of the star sleuth's psychology. 'And what *I*'m going to do is this. Take a big chance, sit tight and wait for him to move: try to plant it here like I've explained. Then, if *you* two co-operate like you've promised, I get him *and* I get the box back and the reward!'

'What have I promised?' asked the girl with trust and deep anxiety in her eyes.

'More than perhaps you realize,' said her father.

Edward enfolded her with a truly loving arm. 'It's quite simple to explain,' he said, 'and if you come out with me in the garden I'll put you in the picture and fill in all the details for you. It's just one or two things that might look wrong, I admit, if it was any other girl than you who did them or anyone else who asked you to do them other than myself. But things, as you'll see, that are very necessary to us for our salvation.'

MR LOVE

A voice behind Frankie as the barber went to get hot towels said softly, 'Hullo, ponce!'

He didn't move an inch because it might be someone else the

voice referred to or, if it was to him, he was a good professional, and
in any case a *man* doesn't let a stranger see he thinks he may have
been insulted. He looked slowly up at the mirror but could see only
a leg reflected. Then, after interminable business with the towels,
he looked again and saw on the leg's knee a hand holding the
unknown client's snuff-box.

This was too much. He got up, much to the hurt indignation of
the barber who'd far from terminated his ministrations, and turned
to see an extremely ordinary young man who (perhaps because his
very nondescriptness made him the perfect substance for the imprint
of his trade) had, quite unmistakably, COPPER written all over his
body and the soul that looked through his eyes. The snuff-box had
now disappeared, and this person rose, walked outside ahead of
Frankie, strolled on a bit then stopped. Frank followed after.
'Recognize it?' the man said, whipping the thing out again.

'I might do.'

'Ah!' (Almost a sigh).

It was at once evident to Frankie that the danger was not
immediate—for otherwise this cop would have said simply, 'Come
along,'—and yet that in some deeper sense he couldn't fathom the
danger was actually greater than if he'd been arrested on the spot.
The two men stood silent, then the copper said, 'A junior colleague
of mine has turned this in to me.'

'Oh, has he?'

'Yes. There's a reward attached to it, as I dare say you may
have guessed.'

'Oh, is there?'

'But I'm not taking it myself, of course. Because this reward, you
see, is unofficial: and me, I like doing things through channels
according to the book. So I'm turning it in myself to my superiors.'

'Why you tell me all this?'

'I thought you might like to hear it.'

As Frankie well knew, most 'questions' are in reality inverted
statements of the questioner that reveal facts he knows (or doesn't
know—another kind of fact) as much as they may ask for them. So
far, all of his own had been of the neutral, unloaded, noncommittal
kind. But he now could not resist asking one that revealed to the
star sleuth a very great deal indeed (even more than the words, the

tone in which it was uttered)—in fact at this juncture, all he really wanted to know: and that was, 'Why did he turn it in to you, this colleague of yours you mention?'

The star sleuth smiled. 'Got windy, I expect. Shaky. Lost his nerve. Decided this thing was too hot for him to hold and he'd better surrender it and forget about any possible private arrangement.'

Frankie said nothing: but his face, the star sleuth was delighted to observe, wore the expressionless look which in strong men of generous temperament denotes a mounting anger.

'There may be repercussions, naturally,' the star sleuth added.

Frankie stood waiting for something more to happen, but nothing did. He turned and walked off, his loose lithe body unnaturally stiff. The star sleuth saw him hail a taxi.

Then he himself returned to the barber's shop and went to the public telephone. He dialled a Walthamstow number and said would they please pick up the woman he'd mentioned earlier and have her sent over, but if the man showed up not to bother about him at all or answer any questions. The customers in the shop (and the proprietor) made a great show of not listening to this, and after the officer's departure burst into speculative chatter.

MR JUSTICE

THE summons, for Edward, to the office of the Detective-sergeant reached him while he was reading back files in the CID records room. One of Edward's greatest delights since he had won himself this job was to retire, in spare moments, to the records section (presided over by a sour, grizzled, gnomic officer who was pensioned already in all but name) and there read over ancient 'cases'. These dead tales written in the stereotyped language of reports delighted him; and he loved to read into the enormous spaces between their amateur-typed lines, and fill in the wealth of probable, actual details that his imagination and his brief experience suggested to him. 'Sir: I have made discreet enquiries concerning the above-named ...' had, for him, all the childhood fascination of 'Once upon a time'.

These folders, dating back for years (and even more so—could he have but seen them!—the massive stacks of antique files assembled in steel cabinets at faraway headquarters), confirmed his belief that within the Force there is guarded and enshrined a principle which is eternal: that power is given by societies to enforce their order in a state of secrecy. Secrecy, order and might, for Edward, were almost holy things and all admirable *in themselves*. And of their dignity and virtue, the files and manuals and card-indexes were the sacred books that he revered.

Indeed, it was not enough to say of Edward—as might be of many excellent men among his colleagues—that he was well-qualified to be a copper: that he had strength, common-sense, intuition, and obedience to hallowed ritual and his superiors. These of themselves would have made him a man marked out for good and worthy things. But Edward possessed two rarer qualities that made his senior officers (as abbots might, or generals of an Order) observe him closely: a moral sense which, though strong, was entirely empirical and would draw its strength uncritically from the institution that he served; more precious still, an attitude towards the Force which could be described without mockery or a great exaggeration, as mystical. Powerful, secret orders of whatever kind attract such men: and the lay Force in this respect was no exception.

It caused, therefore, the Detective-sergeant (who'd recognized in Edward a man of the same qualities, but far greater potential gifts than he possessed himself) some pain to see so born a novice do such foolish things. And being old in the Force and not far from retirement (and so already almost beyond ambition), the Detective-sergeant had decided that if he could, he'd give this young postulant the penances and scourgings which alone at a critical time of his novitiate might save a born copper for the Cause. He looked up from his typewriter, told Edward severely to sit down, remorselessly banged on his page to its conclusion then whipped it out and said, 'Now look, son, this won't do. I've had more than one complaint about you.'

'Sir?'

'Yes, *sir*: several. The first is this: a telegram of all things. Take a look at it, please, and tell me just what it means.'

Edward did. 'It's evidently, sir,' he said, 'an ill-wisher who's hinting I've been staying at the flat in Kilburn with my girl I told you of already.'

'And you have been *staying* there? I mean as man and wife?'

'Yes, sir. But that's over now. She's back with her father, sir, until he goes away.'

'With her father? Going away?'

'Yes, sir. My girl's father's emigrating, and I wanted to consult you about that, sir, if I may.'

'One thing at a time. Now what about this?'

The Detective-sergeant had lifted the plastic cover of his typewriter to reveal, sitting on his potent but unglamorous desk, the snuff-box.

Instantly and calmly (for which the Detective-sergeant gave him points) Edward said, 'I've never seen that thing yet in my life, sir.'

'No?'

'But I shall tell you all I know about it.'

'I'm listening. I might tell *you* I've had it checked for prints . . .'

'You won't find mine, sir. But you might find my girl's.'

The Detective-sergeant covered it once more with the moulded plastic box. 'As a matter of fact,' he said, 'we didn't find anybody's: it's been wiped.'

This brief respite (for which Edward gave the Detective-sergeant no points) enabled Edward rapidly to readjust his theory. 'I'm not surprised to hear it's been wiped, sir,' he said steadily, 'if I'm right about who I think last had it and turned it in to you.'

'Go on . . .' said his superior.

'A colleague of mine, sir,' Edward said, his voice rising slightly (for after all, what harm *had* he done to the star sleuth? His indignation was entirely authentic), 'who saw fit to interfere in a case you gave me that I was handling in my own way one hundred per cent according to regulations, as I understand them.'

'Go on . . .' said the Detective-sergeant.

Edward now told his tale. Experience and native wit had taught him that the closer your story adheres to the truth the more convincing it will sound, and the more difficult it will be to demolish; and that having decided on a story, one must tell it (whatever it may be) with complete assurance and conviction.

His tale tallied with reality in most essential respects. He had visited the ponce Frankie on a tip-off from the Madam, and suggested he'd better find the box, or else. The ponce Frankie who, presumably, had recovered it from his woman, had later given it to Edward's girl, fearing, probably, to hand it to Edward personally. During his girl's absence from her flat the box had been purloined by, he suspected, the star sleuth.

'Why do you think *he* took it?' said the Detective-sergeant.

'Well, sir,' said Edward, risking a throw, '—didn't he?'

The Detective-sergeant smiled slightly. 'Yes. As a matter of fact, he did.'

'And why did he say he did, sir?'

'We'll come to that ... Meanwhile, I'd like to go over your story once again. You got this box from the ponce, you say—or your girl did. Was it your intention to turn it in?'

'Of course, sir.'

'You hadn't any other plans for it?'

'Such as what, sir?'

'I'll do the questioning. And if you thought this ponce or else his whore, which are one and the same thing, had got the box, you didn't think of searching their place for it?'

'I hadn't a warrant, sir.'

'You don't need a warrant if there's strong suspicion of a felony. You didn't know *that*? And you didn't think of *arresting* anybody?'

'I had no evidence of theft, sir.'

'Or of consulting me or *anyone* as to procedure?' Edward was silent. 'And tell me constable, please. Why haven't I heard of all this from you before?'

'Look, sir! Put yourself in my position, please. I get the box—or my girl does. Then it disappears. I think I know *who's* taken it, and I think I know *why*. But how could I prove that to you, sir, or to anyone, until this man who stole it from me did whatever I thought he was going to do?'

'And what was that?'

'Make some use of it to harm me, sir.'

The Detective-sergeant looked at his protégé, head on one side, then said, 'If there's one thing I detest here in the Force, it's personal feuds mixed up with what's supposed to be our duties.'

Edward slightly hung his head and said, 'Yes, sir.'

'And secrets among ourselves, so that you don't know who in the Force knows what.'

Edward still bowed his head.

'Avoid it yourself, then. Now. The report I have when this thing was handed to me, is that it was confiscated from you when it was found you hadn't turned it in yourself immediately as you should have done. Now . . .' the senior officer raised (as if halting a two-ton truck) a hand ' . . . I'll be checking up on both your stories and I'd like a word, please, very early, with that girl of yours. Is she on the phone?'

'Yes, sir. At her father's place, she is.'

'Very well. Please ask her to step round. Now for you, we've got work for you: I want you to get a statement from the girl.'

'Which girl, sir?'

'The ponce's: the girl that stole this little object, as we've reason to believe.'

'I'd have to find her, sir.'

'You'll find her in the cells.'

'Sir?'

'We've brought her in.'

'Here, sir?'

'That's what I say.'

'And the man too?'

'No: I want you to pick him up when you've had a go at the woman who kept him in tobacco.'

'But, sir . . . who nicked her?'

The Detective-sergeant looked with kindly irony at his junior. 'I do wish,' he said, 'you younger constables would *not* use slang terms when you're on duty. It was your colleague that arrested her: the one you say has got a down on you.'

'And he hasn't questioned her, then, sir?'

'No.'

'Why?'

'Look, son. *You're* asking *me* a great many questions. He hasn't questioned her because he's lying on his bed.'

'Why, sir?'

'Why? Because he's gone sick, and our doctor has okayed it. Ulcers, he says, he's had them before—though I must say I thought only old men like me were entitled to convenient illnesses when there's a bit of work to finish.' The detective rose. 'However,' he continued, 'that's how it is: so get down to the cells, please, and see what the painted lady's got to say.'

Edward rose also, and hesitating (or seeming to) said, speaking suddenly rather fiercely, 'Sir, I hope when my girl comes here you'll remember that she's pregnant.'

'Oh—ho! And how can I remember that if I didn't know it? Well! You've been cutting things a bit fine, haven't you?'

'I'm hoping, sir, my application for a marriage permit will go through quite quickly.'

'It had better, sonny, hadn't it. Well, get on down.'

MR LOVE

FINDING his girl was gone and that he himself had not yet been molested, Frankie experienced the most unpleasant of anxieties— the sensation of being *conditionally* free: of knowing that sooner or later at some unexpected moment the tap might come upon his shoulder (or, to modernize the metaphor, the twist might come upon his biceps). No state is more unnerving: which is the reason why the Force sometimes lays in wait before it pounces.

There had also been a most unpleasant session with his girl's faith-healing Mum when he had called at Walthamstow and found the old girl prostrated. As his girl's Mum saw it ... what on earth was a ponce *for* if not to get arrested—if arrest there must be— *instead* of the girl he batted on? To the ancient wrath of an *ad hoc* mother-in-law towards her daughter's companion was added an out-raged sense of what was, professionally, appropriate.

In this confusion Frankie recalled a skipper's maxim about what to do if the ship was overtaken by a hurricane. However urgent the case·may seem (this old mariner had said), and however thick and black the clouds may gather, before you *do* anything take a few minutes off, at least, and *think*.

This Frankie did in a back room at the Bengali's house in Stepney, for he'd already decided not to set foot again at Kilburn in any circumstances. He reflected on what he might owe to his girl—in the sense of loyalty—and decided he owed nothing: she'd used him, and would have dropped him if need be; he'd used her, and now he would do the same. That was the deal their life together had been based on, and now the deal was over. He'd miss her, yes, and those dawn sessions, but that was all part of being 'in business'. So now he would cut out, leave her, 'the game', and England too for quite a while.

Only two things troubled Frankie slightly about this analysis: that the girl had been knocked off for doing something which—essentially, if not technically—she had not done, that is, helping herself to the fucking snuff-box. Still, he'd done his best to straighten that out for her and she'd been a bloody fool ever to accept it.

The other thing was this mean-minded bastard who had shopped her. He'd done all the cop had asked—got him back the box so that he could collect . . . well anyway, although admittedly he'd stacked it on the girl to try to scare the pair of them away, they'd *got* the thing and him, he'd kept his mouth shut about the whole performance: whereupon this treacherous sod had turned it in and told them to knock off *his* girl. He'd like to *get* that copper, he decided: but though revenge was sweet, freedom was sweeter, and the thing to do now was get aboard a plane.

MR JUSTICE

EDWARD's interrogation of the ponce Frankie's girl had been brief and colourful. Yelling at him and calling him improper names (so that he'd had to summon the assistance of a copperess, a thing no male cop likes doing), she'd stuck to her story that the box had been a gift freely given, and when asked about her ponce had said she'd never used the monsters—and if they thought she'd got one why didn't they try to find him?

She further volubly made a point that seemed to Edward (as it might well do to many reasonable persons) a very good one: if they doubted her story, why didn't they go and ask the distinguished client who had given the box to her? Why did they always go for the girls and never for the men who prostituted them? Well—mark her words—they'd better: because if they brought this case against her she'd bloody well have this client subpoenaed—even if she had to use an Asian or an African lawyer who wouldn't be afraid of going for a colleague in the legal profession.

Left to himself Edward, of course, would have turned the girl loose, restored the box rewardless to the Madam, and have forgotten as rapidly as might be about the business. But now this was impossible: the star sleuth's report was in, and his own position, in relation to his girl, was poised in a delicate, precarious state of crisis. No: the only thing to do was ram home the charge quick and try to make it stick and get this bloody woman out of the way. As for the ponce, if he had any sense he'd skip, and Edward wouldn't try all that much to hinder him: although, to comply with the direct order of the Detective-sergeant, he must now go through the motions of trying to find Frankie.

To do so he knew it would be pointless, almost, to go to Frankie's Kilburn flat (at any rate initially), and he decided instead to conduct his faint-hearted pursuit through the medium of the star ponce. Although this man's name was not yet known to him, from enquiries among his colleagues, and a glance through the photographic albums, he was soon identified; and armed with sufficient damaging particulars to force the star ponce, unless he was an imbecile, to betray his friend, Edward set out for the drinking-club where the star and his colleagues were well known to foregather.

The news of the arrest of Frankie's girl had already spread by the ponce-prostitute bush telegraph to the confines of the club (rather as, in Pall Mall, a disaster to a senior civil servant would be known long before it hit an inside bottom column of the top people dailies). Edward, who (unlike several of his colleagues) was not a member of the club and thus not entitled to buy drinks there, adopted the sensible and conventionally acceptable tactic of going straight up to the bar (followed by twenty-eight or so pairs of eyes) and saying, 'I'm an officer on a routine check-up. I wonder if you'd let me have a drink?' This was instantly forthcoming (his offer of payment being accepted, with a slight smile, as the politer of the two alternatives), and holding the beer glass like a shield, Edward took a slow look round the room.

Seated with an air of bland wariness and attired in a superb Italianate confection which accented, just sufficiently, the superb formation of his limbs, the star ponce lightly held a brandy glass with a slim, solid hand on whose wrist delicately dangled a thin gold chain. Like two who have an unspoken agreement for a rendezvous, the ponce and Edward Justice now came together.

Edward explained that all he wanted from the ponce was this: to lead him to Frankie Love. The ponce, after suggesting, helpfully, the Kilburn flat and appearing surprised that Edward should think Frankie might not be there, said courteously that he was very sorry, he could be of no further assistance to the officer.

Edward half sighed, put down his glass, and bringing his face closer to the ponce's said very softly, 'Look, I'm sorry too, son, but it's this way. The heat's on at the station to find this boy, I've got to make an effort to do so, and you're the only man I know in town I've ever seen him with. So don't you see until I get hold of him, I'll just have to hold on to you. And I do mean hold, son. I've been looking up your file just recently, and I'd say you're about due for another spell inside. So it really is up to you to help me in my enquiries if you want to avoid anything of that nature—which, and I do mean this, would happen to you *immediately* if you don't.'

'Officer,' the star ponce said, 'I'm really very sorry but I don't know where this boy is and I cannot help you.'

Edward smiled, sighed again, got up and said, 'Well, come along.'

Not rising, and raising his voice slightly so that it could be heard at neighbouring tables, the star ponce said, 'Are you *arresting* me, officer?'

'That, we'll see.'

'No, I mean *now*. Because if you're not arresting me and bringing a charge against me that you think can stick, then I'm sorry, but I'm just not coming: not coming, I mean, merely to help you in your enquiries I know nothing of.'

'You're under arrest,' said Edward sadly.

'For what?'

'Suspected collusion. Assisting a wanted person in an attempt to evade arrest . . .'

One could have heard an ice-cube drop. Nobody moved, everybody watched.

'Dear!' said the star ponce to the girl behind the bar. 'Will you make a few phone calls for me, please?'

The girl nodded, the star ponce rose (looking more glorious even than when seated), and the pair departed amid a silence distilled of hatred, fear and alcohol.

Edward hailed a cab, and on the journey to the station neither man said a word—except over the paraphernalia of cigarette lighting. For the cigarette, in the twentieth century, is often the ultimate offering of deadly enemies just prior to a fatal issue.

At the station Edward parked the ponce in a small room for twenty minutes chiefly to let him 'get the atmosphere'. The star ponce shrank gradually and visibly, and his splendid clothes (like elegant mufti on a raw recruit) became increasingly inappropriate to their setting. In spirit, however, the ponce, who'd seen all this before, remained calm and buoyant.

Then Edward collected two colleagues skilled in these matters (always take two—for safety and as witnesses of each other) and removed the star ponce to a distant cell. As the door clinked to, Edward made his final, reasonable appeal. 'Feller,' he said, 'here is the spiel. You take me to this boy and that ends that. If not, you're going to leave this place just crunched a bit though unmarked in any way that will be proveable; furthermore I promise you a poncing charge, with all the trimmings, within twenty-four hours from this very moment.'

Inwardly in his turn, the star ponce sighed. It wasn't that he was a coward: not in a fight, anyway; and even unarmed and sober—unlike so many of the boys. But if they'd got the heat turned that hot on poor old Francis they'd get him even if they waited fifty years. He looked at the three officers—Edward watching him earnestly, the other two eyeing him with frank amusement—and he said, 'I'm not going to make a statement, officer. And whatever you may say I've said in court I shall deny it, please understand. All I'm prepared to do is this: give me a piece of paper and I'll write an address on it: that's all.'

'Very well,' said Edward, handing to the star essential stationery. The two colleagues stood back a bit bored by this development, as the star ponce inscribed block capitals. Edward took back the book, looked at it carefully, said thank you and signalled his colleagues to open the door and go.

The star ponce also stood. 'I'm in the clear?' he said.

'No,' Edward said calmly. 'You'll stay here for just a little while.'

The door closed and the star ponce subsided on the wooden bench-cum-bed with the built-in lavatory pan.

MR LOVE

AWAITING the departure of his plane which left late at night, but sure somehow already that he wouldn't be on it, Frankie went out into Stepney to have a drink: both because his Mahometan host didn't keep alcohol and Frankie disapproved of Indian hemp (well, just didn't like it), and because he was determined, even at the risk of being caught, that he wasn't going to *hide* from anyone: be very careful, yes, and use his loaf, but not lose his self-respect by *lurking*.

In Stepney the licensing hours, though their existence is politely recognized, are dexterously evaded in a number of cordial speak-easies: where after the club below has closed at the well-regulated hour with much clanging of bolts and ritual cries of, 'Last orders, please!' selected guests proceed to upper rooms to eat, drink, embrace their girls or gamble. To such an establishment Frankie now repaired and was soon ensconced beside a whisky bottle in a second-floor room, and in the company of various citizens of the outlying countries of the British Commonwealth of nations.

Here his meal of chicken-and-peas was interrupted by an insistent summons, from the proprietor, to a public call-box insalubriously situated beside an appalling bi-sexual lavatory. The voice at the far end, agitated and thus more incomprehensible than usual, was that of the excellent Bengali: who told him 'one law man' had called at the house just after he'd left and made enquiries concerning him; that he, the Bengali, had revealed absolutely nothing and the law man had now departed; and that Frankie must take 'well care' not to return to the house as 'the eye' was certainly put upon it; and finally—in a torrent of the most urgent assurance—whatever happened he, Frankie, could absolutely rely on him, the Bengali, to safeguard all his property and hide it: as he had already done with his packed travelling bag by stuffing it, the very moment he'd heard the untoward soft knock, inside the communal dust-bin out the back.

Frankie expressed thanks and assured his friend of his total belief in his integrity (he meant this). He then hung up and without returning to the festive communal room went quickly downstairs to the street. At the door he tapped himself to check on the presence of his passport and his money: the luggage, such as it was, could be abandoned.

He set off through the Stepney streets but in an *easterly* direction. What they'd be expecting him to do, he calculated, was go to the West end of the city to an air terminal. Instead he'd make for London docks, try to get a ride or even stow away, and if he failed travel overland to an eastern port and reach the Continent of Europe. Ships, after all, were his affair and more reliable. Diagnosing thus he saw again, approaching on the further pavement and this time on night duty, the young officer who had arrested him, earlier on, over the absurdity of the bag.

In their feeling for persons they have succeeded in convicting, the officers of the Force fall into three chief types. There are those who feel that any convicted person is a 'client' who should return from time to time for treatment: if you do harm to a man, you should prove how right you were by harming him again. Then those who feel in an almost friendly fashion, well, he's done his lot, good luck to him, he's stale stuff now, let's look round for someone else. And then those (a very minor group) who just feel nothing in particular: it was 'a case'.

Unfortunately the officer now approaching Frankie belonged to category one; and recognizing his former victim (though regretting that on this occasion he didn't appear to be carrying a suspect bag) he crossed the road obliquely (and warily, too), his boots sounding like metal (as was indeed the case), and there he stopped a few feet from the pavement by which Frankie was advancing, in as safe-and-sound a position as seemed possible for the encounter.

But this time Frankie knew the danger; and approaching steadily as if he saw nothing untoward, he suddenly hurled all the small change in his pocket at the copper's face, turned abruptly down one of the eighteenth-century courts which in this section of Stepney intricately abound, and loped off fairly silently yet at considerable speed. A whistle blew, a torch shone, and feet came clanging.

Without much difficulty Frankie outwitted his pursuer by entering, while still some way ahead, one of the bombed buildings which, a generation after the end of World War II, still rot and crumble in the capital; and there he settled himself quickly down upon a pile of fairly comfortable rubble and abandoned furniture that lay timelessly dissolving in a distant corner.

'Fuck off!' said a voice.

Quite unaware, Frankie had stumbled on what was to the detritus of the floating population of the borough, their trysting-place; and the position he had selected within a few feet of those who in more pastoral surroundings might be described as a 'courting couple'. This couple clearly wanted to get on with their courting without uncouth interruption.

'Take it easy, mate,' said Frankie softly. 'I got to stay here a moment.'

The male—who by his tones and truculence Frankie observed to his dismay was drunk—repeated, 'I said, fuck off. You got no respect for privacy?'

Frankie risked a throw. 'You a seaman like I am?' he said.

'No!'

It *would* be a landsman. Frankie tried again. 'You like a pound-note, mate? I got to stay here a while—it's a bit urgent.'

From the rubble and his invisible (though audibly grunting) consort, the erotic landsman rose like an angry phoenix. 'Now, look!' he cried very much too loud for Frankie's liking. 'Just make away or I have to thump you.'

Frankie got up, biting his rage, said, 'Okay, mate,' and started slowly towards the light. Unwisely from every point of view the landsman tried to help him on his way with a parting shove. Consequently both men stumbled, and several hundredweight of miscellaneous London ruins and garbage collapsed with a resounding, thudding clatter.

A bit bashed on the head and dazed, Frankie staggered up knee-deep in obstacles as several lights came on in surrounding buildings, accompanied by cries and sleepy murmurs. As he struggled to the exit a torch shone blank-flash in his face—a startling experience at the best of times. Ten minutes later, filthy and rather battered, he was lodged in the adjacent headquarters of the Force where an interested sergeant was examining his passport and several envelopes crammed with currency.

MR JUSTICE

EDWARD, having done his duty—no more, no less—by tracing Frankie to his Stepney hide-out, and after taking the routine precaution of warning the local station that a wanted man was now at large among them, had returned to his own headquarters to draw up a nil report and—an even more pressing matter—discover what had passed, if anything, between his girl and the all too astute Detective-sergeant.

She was waiting for him in her eternally patient way amid the bleak décor of the junior officers' canteen. He sat down opposite her beneath a single shaft of strip-light, and with two coffees in paper cups from the automatic urn. 'Well, dear, let's hear what,' he said.

'The Detective-sergeant believes your story.'

'How? What?'

'The story you told him, Ted dear. That you were going to hand in the box and hadn't even had a chance to see it before it was stolen from me.'

'And what did he say about the man who stole it?'

'Nothing. No, we didn't mention him at all.'

'So he's satisfied I've done no wrong.'

'About that, he is ... But, Edward. Now, dearest, *don't* be angry with me—but he got it out of me.'

'Got what?'

'He said it was for your good in your career, and mine.'

'What did you *say*? Tell me *what.*'

'About Dad: he knows Dad has a previous conviction.'

'Yes? Oh.'

'He asked me if *I* had and I said of course not, and he said he believed me though he'd check, but there's one thing he doesn't like about it.'

'That *I* didn't tell him, I suppose.'

'Yes: and that you *did* tell him I was a copper-hater and not that my father's been in jail. Did you really have to do that, Ted?'

'I'm sorry, dear. I'm very sorry—that was a big mistake. I was harassed and . . . well, I made a big mistake.'

'Yes, Ted. Another one you made, it seems, was to tell *me* you'd told him that you had no girl at all.'

'But he doesn't know I said that to you . . .'

'No, Ted, I know: it was only to me you lied.'

'Yes. Dearing, I'm sorry—do try to understand! But him. Was he very vexed when he discovered?'

'Not so much about that, Ted . . . about something else. That you made me pregnant before you got the whole thing settled.'

'Well! What business is that of his?'

'He said it was for two reasons, Edward. First, that he didn't like it because it wasn't right to me. Then . . .'

'To you! What does he care about you?'

'Well, Edward, I agree with him.'

'Oh, do you!'

'Yes—I do. I think he's right. He was like a father to me, Ted.'

'A father! If you only knew him! Well, what was the other thing?'

'Well, dear, you won't like this, but he says your application *may* go through if Dad leaves fairly soon, but it *won't* if I have a child before we marry, and he doesn't see us being able to do that before the application is approved.'

'It takes that long?'

'He says so.'

Edward looked at her. 'Well, there's only one thing,' he said, 'you'll have to have a miscarriage.'

His girl looked back. 'I don't want to now, Edward.'

'But you said you were willing to.'

'I did, yes, but I've thought of it, and it's got so much bigger here, and Ted, I'm going to have my baby.'

'Oh, you are.'

'Yes.'

He reached for her hands across the table, delved for them and held them. 'Darling,' he said, 'do think of this. If you have the child it seems I've got to choose between the Force and you.'

'I know,' she said. 'I've thought of that.'

'And what do you expect me to do?'

'You've got to decide, Ted. I suppose it all depends on how much you think you love me.'

Another shaft of the strip-light came on as an officer, entering suddenly, called out, 'It's okay, Ted—we've got him.'

MR LOVE AND MR JUSTICE

EDWARD was now faced by that most exhausting and complicated moment in a copper's life—the conduct of a full-scale interrogation of a prisoner. In this affair both parties have considerable tactical advantages, provided each knows what they are and how to use them.

First, the surroundings. The very word 'cells' has, to most ears, a sinister and forbidding ring. And these places are, to be sure, rebarbative enough ... the nastiest thing about them being not that they have locks and bars, but that they are so utterly, fundamentally *utilitarian*. In them arrangements are made for prisoners to eat, sleep, and defecate: and for absolutely nothing else whatever. A man in prison is reduced to his physical essence.

From the copper's point of view the cells have the advantage, obviously, of making escape impossible to the prisoner and of filling his soul with lonely terror and foreboding. But they have this psychological *dis*advantage that in one very real sense, they are the prisoner's and not the copper's home: yes, home. The copper may lord it in his office, and of course does so over any visitor he may entice there. But in the cells the visitor in one sense is *he*, the copper, even though he has put the prisoner inside them. And if the prisoner be a man of intelligence, will and courage, the very presence of these four confining walls does help to sustain his spirits. It is he who is on the defensive, he who is fighting back. And he may well detect in even the most arrogant aggression of the interrogating copper, a hidden fear of the place of a very different kind from his own: the fear of something with which in the most final sense, he is unfamiliar.

When it comes to the actual interrogation the copper has, of course, the enormous advantage of seeming to personify the fact of prison itself, and the whole vast Force of which he is the representative. He will also possess, through skill and long practice, all the interrogator's essential arts in which the prisoner may be quite unversed. But: in this very unfamiliarity, there resides also a great strength. An adult questioning a child about a misdemeanour often finds himself exhausted by his own superior guile, and defeated by the instinctive simplicities of the apparently weaker party in the struggle. So it may be said to be with prisoners. And they also have —once again if men of indomitable stamp—one absolutely unbeatable trump card which is the fact that they *are*, in this circumstance, alone. If you are alone, you can never be betrayed; and in dealing with the many others who may confront him, the prisoner is the only person among the whole assembly who really knows *all* that everyone has said and done.

Frankie's opening gambit to his captor Edward, was in the finest tradition of the pugnacious victim: 'You're a nice bastard,' he said, as Edward carefully closed the cell door behind him.

Edward smiled slightly and looked interrogative.

'I gave you the way out,' Frankie continued, 'I gave your girl the box and all you had to do was to collect. And then you shop me. Why?'

'It's not quite as you think,' said Edward carefully—doubly so because he was keeping an eye on Frankie for sudden violence, and had his whistle handy.

'Oh, no?' said Frankie. 'Go on—tell me your fairytale.'

'What happened,' Edward said, 'is that a senior of mine who doesn't like me got hold of the box and turned it in, and made things very awkward for me, too, I can tell you.'

'For you! Well, listen to that! I dunno, son! You coppers really are a bunch of horrors.'

'You think so?'

'Yes, man, I do. A bunch of narks in uniform.

'Have a fag,' said Edward.

' "Have a fag! Have a fag!" Listen—skip it, *officer*. Now, tell me. What's the charge?'

'There may be several.'

'Thank you! And there may be lawyers, too! And some bloody expensive ones! I'd just like to make that clear. And there may be an affidavit about your visit to me—*with* a witness present, don't forget. No one will believe two ponces, I'm well aware of that, but it won't sound very nice up in the Sessions—because that's where we're going, let me tell you, you're not getting away with a magistrate's court and no publicity.'

'I understand how you feel,' Edward said.

'You kill me, son. Honest you do! And what about this tale of yours? Why *should* a *colleague* of yours do the dirty on you?'

'Don't you see?'

'I think I do: you've invented the whole dam thing.'

'No. No, I haven't. The reason my colleague made it difficult for me was that he hoped you'd do exactly what you're doing now— and that is attack me.'

'You're saying I've laid *hands* on you? Is that what you're concocting now?'

'This man hoped you would, once you thought I'd deceived you.'

'You ask me to believe that?'

'No, not particularly: I'm just telling you what happened.'

Frankie accepted, nevertheless, the ritual fag. 'The Force!' he said quietly. 'The Force! I really feel pity for you all. And if all that's so,' he continued, 'why did you come down chasing after me to Stepney?'

'I didn't.'

'Listen . . .'

'*You* listen, please. I didn't *chase* after you. I checked at your address because it was the very least I could do. Then I came back here and made no further enquiries. It's *you*, isn't it, who's got yourself foolishly arrested through no fault of mine.'

'You didn't send that bastard out looking for me?'

'I sent no one. It was your own carelessness that caused it, as you must know.'

'Thank you! And what happens now? You still holding my girl?'

'Yes.'

'And you're going to bring charges against us both—is that it?'

Edward now sat down on the bench-cum-lavatory and said to Frankie, 'Please do listen to me. I'm not asking you to do anything I say because that's your business, obviously. But I am asking you, please, just to listen.'

Frankie sat down too. 'Very well,' he said. 'I'm listening.'

'From my point of view,' said Edward carefully, '—and I *do* wish you'd realize this—the lighter you and your girl get off the better I'll be pleased.'

'Why? You like us?'

'Do please just *listen*. Because now that the box has been turned in, the less said about my part in trying to recover it the better.'

'Yeah. Corruption and bribery. Very nasty. My heart bleeds for you.'

'On the other hand,' Edward continued, 'if you and your girl *don't* want to help me, well, in for a penny in for a pound, I may as well help press the charge hard and get you both sent away as long as possible.'

Frankie looked sideways at Edward. 'You know,' he said, 'if you'd had any sense you'd have offered to split the price of the box with me, and just said you couldn't trace it.'

'I might have done,' said Edward, also looking sideways, 'if you'd seen me alone and not been so damned unpleasant and suspicious.'

'Yes, I see what you mean. It's a great pity. You could have bought yourself a nice new fridge, and I'd have bought myself some valuable protection.'

'Well, there it is,' said Edward. 'The thing's now as it is. Now, I'm asking you for no promises: I'm not a fool. But all I will say to you is *if* you leave out the part about my not wanting to turn it in—which no one will believe much anyway—then I'll say I believe your girl thought she had it as a present, and that you offered to co-operate with the authorities.'

'Yeah?'

'Yes. Now, I don't ask you to credit this, of course, before you see it happen. But I would point out this. I'm willing to take a chance on you that you don't have to at all on me. Prosecution evidence comes first at any trial and can't be altered afterwards. When your turn comes to speak, you can make it dependent on whatever it is you hear me say.'

Frankie threw his fag-end in the pan and pressed the automatic flush which sounded off like six Niagaras. 'Well obviously,' he said when the waters had subsided, 'I'll think that over. And that's really all I'm going to say just now.'

'I can't ask for more. Another fag?'

'Well, I don't mind. What about bail? What are the chances?'

'Oh, quite good, I'd say, for *one* of you at any rate . . .'

'What does that mean?'

'Well, we've got to bring a charge of theft: you do understand that, don't you? Unless we hear the owner—the original owner of the thing—saying to us it was a gift, then a charge must lay. But it needn't necessarily be on both of you.'

'Who will it be on?'

'The girl.'

'Why?'

'Look. *You* didn't sleep with this man, did you?'

'Take it easy, son, or I may smack you. And what about me?'

'Aiding and abetting—but *with*, of course, my favourable statement, in certain circumstances, coming later . . . and a charge against you might even not be made.'

'And no bail for my girl: is that it?'

'Well, it's up to the magistrate: but I'd say probably no.'

'I see.'

They smoked a moment in silence. Then Frankie said, 'You're shacked up with one too, aren't you?'

'Yes . . . You know I am.'

'I might have something to say to the court about *that* as well.'

'You'd be wasting your breath. She's already told everything to my superiors.'

'Why?'

'It came up as a result of all this: on account of you giving *her* the box, and not me as you should have done if you'd had any sense at all.'

'Dear, dear, dear. So I've landed *you* in the shit, too! Well, well. You like that girl?'

'I want to marry her.'

'You do? Now why? Is that a thing coppers do?'

'Because I love her.'

'You believe in that crap, son?'

'Yes.'

'Not just sex?'

'Without love there is no sex.'

'Well! And you tell *me* that!'

Edward paused then said, 'You won't mind my saying so, I hope, but I think what you do is just disgusting. *Not* because it's illegal—don't misunderstand me. But because it destroys the best thing there is in any man and woman.'

' "Not because it's illegal"! You don't believe in the law, then?'

'Of course I do. But the law isn't perfect and entire like love can be.'

Frankie arose. 'Well, are you *sure* of that?' he said. 'Because me I've found it's women and sex that are imperfect—just a game. But as for the law—if it's a *real* law, a true law like you get on board a ship, why! then it's really something! A thing you can respect and live for.'

'I don't know about ships,' said Edward, 'naturally. But here on land it's all made up of human beings struggling with one another, and that means imperfection. There are rules, of course, and they're mostly very clear: laws that have been laid down for centuries, I mean. But there's no such thing as *law*, like there is love.'

'Well, son. You may be right, of course, but I think you're wrong. There's three laws in the world here as I see it: the rules you speak of, the way you bastards alter and interpret them, and then—way on beyond and right in the centre of things—there's just . . . the *law*.'

Edward got up too. 'I don't really know,' he said, 'what you're talking about.'

'You may not,' said Frankie Love. 'Because if you did, you wouldn't be a copper.'

'Well,' Edward said, smiling a bit sourly. 'I may *not* be one before all that long, any more.'

'Oh? You retiring on your winnings?'

'No. My girl's pregnant, and the Force may not let me marry her.'

'You've not thought of an abortion?'

'She doesn't want one.'

'Good for her! She's too good for a copper—tell her so from me. And to marry her you'd have to resign?'

'It looks like that.'

'You're a fool, mate. No woman's worth a job—even yours—if your heart's in it.'

'Well, I don't know. I may stay on.'

'And if you do, and she has the kid, she loses you?'

'Yes.'

'And she cares for you, this woman?'

'Yes.'

'Well yes, she's quite a girl! She really is. I must try and get her away from you when I get out.'

'You'd better look after your own, hadn't you? It's she who'll be needing you—not mine.'

'What does that one mean?'

'If you get bail I suppose you'll try to skip, won't you?'

'*You* ask me to tell *you* that?'

'Yes, but I don't ask you for an answer . . .'

'So what should I do, according to you? Stay and try to take the rap for her? Say I forced her to pinch the thing or something lunatic like that?'

'That's what she's quite ready to do for you.'

'What d'you say?'

'When I saw her earlier on she said she was only prepared to make a statement if you weren't implicated.'

'*She* said *that*?'

'Yes.'

'Look—I don't believe you.'

'Ask her some time.'

'She really did say that?'

'I'm telling you.'

'Well, I'll be fucked! Well, I bloody well never!'

In the surprise of his emotion Frankie turned, spontaneously, to make brief use of the adjacent pan. This action transmitted (as is its wont) a similar desire to Edward, who after a casual 'You don't mind?' followed his prisoner's example.

'Well, well, well, well!' said Frankie. 'These chicks! They're packed with surprises!'

'They certainly are,' Edward said reflectively. 'They do things that impress you—even the worst of them.'

'You're not referring to my girl, I hope—I mean, when you say "worst"?'

'No . . . she's still a woman.'

'She's very much one, let me tell you.'

'I don't doubt your word . . .'

Frankie, in his dishevelled garments, looked at the neatly un-uniformed cop and said, 'I suppose you think that they and we men are a lot of anti-social parasites.'

'Yes. As a matter of fact I do.'

'Just about what we think of you. Isn't that crazy?'

'I suppose so . . .'

'Well, let me tell you one thing, copper. We may be that, but there's one thing we're not which you are, and that's hypocrites puffed up with spiritual pride.'

'I don't see you've got much to be proud of anyway.'

'I said *spiritual* pride. We're free from that, most of us easy-money boys. And I wouldn't change that freedom for your prim self-righteousness!'

Edward said nothing: as matter of fact he was (being very tired) getting a bit bored with Frankie and had decided to bring the inter-view—already somewhat excessively unconventional—to a close.

'Although,' Frankie continued with the passion for conversation induced by even a short stay between four closed walls, 'I dare say you *could* maintain we have one thing in common, you and I: in the upside-down world we both live in we've got a certain kind of free-dom that none of the mugs outside will ever know. Neither of us conforms to the accepted pattern: so that we boys are free in spite of all our heart-beats, as I dare say you are in spite of all your discipline.'

Preparing for his departure, Edward had introduced a more formal note in his demeanour. Frankie noticed this and his tone altered. 'Just one thing, officer,' he said. 'You've not told me how you knew I was at Stepney.'

'No.'

'Well, aren't you going to?'

'No.'

'It wasn't my girl?'

'No.'

'Then the only other person I can think of who did know is the Bengali, who it can't be, or . . . yes! My fellow ponce! Is that it?'

'I'm not telling you.'

'So it *is*. Thanks, I'll remember! And one more thing.' Frankie came close to Edward and said to him, 'I promise you—if I lie, I die—I'll keep your name out of it if you do all you can to free my girl.'

Edward paused and said, 'You've changed your mind about her, then?'

'Not about *her* but about her position. I got her in this mess by making her give me the box, and I ought to get her out if I possibly can. So I want the charge to be put on me and only me. You'll do what you can?'

'I'll try,' said Edward. 'But you'll realize I can't promise.'

MR JUSTICE

EDWARD who with an instinct similar to Frankie's could no longer bear the thought of the Kilburn flat, and who'd decided after his late night up on duty to play truant from the section-house, had camped with the older man's permission at the house of his girl's Dad in Kensal Green. And when he awoke it was to the most delicious of situations—his girl bending over him holding a brimming cuppa, and looking down at him with love and a total preoccupation with their joint well-being. He reached up and hugged her and upset most of the tea.

'I love you, Ted,' she said, reaching an arm backward with the crockery and slops in search of an invisible piece of furniture.

'Me, too. Even more. Listen, dearest. I'm going to have it out with the Detective-sergeant.'

'How, Ted? How can you?'

'Reverse the process: turn the tables on him: go over to the attack. Either he helps me fix our marriage, or all right I resign and he loses a good man.'

'And you think that'll work, dear?'

'It might do. I'm sick of caution and of secrets anyway. What about your Dad? Is he all set to go?'

'Any time now. He says it's up to us to send him the balance he needs as soon as ever we can. If not—well, he says he'll come back.'

'He won't! I'll see to that.'

She'd sat down on the bed. 'I wish, Ted,' she said, 'that just at this moment I felt better.'

'You're not ill are you, dear?' said Edward, gently pressing his hand upon her body.

'A bit: you know how it is for me just now: and today I do feel queer.'

'Step up to the pre-natal clinic, darling. See what they have to say.'

'I mean to.'

He kissed her all over.

'You know, dear,' he said, 'that ponce was most impressed with you making up your mind to keep the baby.'

'He was? I thought they didn't like kids, those people.'

'Well—he's all for female children being born, I dare say. Is that what ours is going to be?'

'No, a boy. Has *his* woman ever had one, then?'

'No, I don't think so. . . . But she's certainly got guts—she stuck to him, and now he's going to stick to her.'

The girl shook her head vaguely, not in denial of what he said but to show how important matters prevented her thinking clearly of whatever he was saying. He kissed her again—neck this time, a favourite spot (women were so tough there, so everlasting yet so fragile and so downy)—then said, 'Out of it, dear, we're not hitched up yet and you know I've never liked you to see me dressing till we are.' She smiled at his prudery, took the cup and went away.

Edward decided not to check in at the section-house, and thus when he reached the station found his colleagues in that state of glee in which colleagues are when one of their number—especially one talented and fairly virtuous—has committed an offence of which he is as yet unaware. 'You're for the high jump,' someone said. 'The Detective-sergeant's been chasing after you all morning.'

When he came into the office, Edward found his superior relatively benign. He was standing by the window, which looked out on nothing, and he turned round to Edward and said, 'Well, there have been developments.'

'Sir?'

'With one man sick and the other—well, a bit involved—I've taken over this whole Madam case myself.'

'Yes, sir . . .'

'Now, from what I can make out this client, this eminent individual who the bloody box belongs to (the officer showed some dentures in a rather ghastly grin), thinking—and he's quite right—he might get involved himself in court proceedings, is going to make no charge and in fact is going further—he's going to say he *did* give the girl the snuff-box. These were only the Madam's words, and I'll check of course, but I've no doubt she's got full authority for them from her principal.'

'Well! He's caused us a lot of trouble over nothing, sir.'

'Hasn't he just! The public's *always* calling us in in a tizzy and then when we get their man for them refusing to co-operate in a prosecution.'

'So that puts the pair of them in the clear, sir?'

'I'm coming to that . . . But first of all, my lad, a word in *your* little red ear. The Madam also says you offered to get the box back for a bribe: "reward" she called it. But I prefer "bribe". Well?'

'I've nothing to say, sir.'

'That was correct?'

'Yes, sir.'

'Why you do this, son?'

'I needed money, sir: to help my girl's father emigrate like I told you.'

'You needed money! Really, lad, you *are* a bloody fool! You really *are*!' The Detective-sergeant looked at him. 'With a man like our colleague suffering with his ulcers on the same case with you, you thought you'd under-cut him? A sharp bastard like that? Really! Have you *no* brains in your head at all?'

'I think I'm learning, sir.'

'Well, I do hope so. Now, please in the future *do* be sensible and don't be greedier than your rank and length of service warrants.'

'No, sir.'

'Right. That's forgotten, then. You understand me?'

'Thank you, sir. Thank you very much indeed.'

'Okay. Now, as to the thieves who are no longer thieves. I'm turning the girl loose as I've nothing to hold her on. But I'm going to bring a charge against the man.'

'What charge, sir?'

'What do you think, son? Poncing. He's about due for his first experience and it might as well be now.'

'Excuse me, sir. Who will you get for witnesses? I don't think the girl will speak against him . . .'

'For witnesses? Well, I can think of two . . . Our friend the star sleuth, when he recovers, will be number one and number two, lad, will be you.'

'Me, sir?'

'Naturally. You've both kept observation on the flat—in fact you, you've been living on the doorstep—you've both seen clients come and go and there'll just be the little matter of saying that on several occasions you saw her hand him over considerable sums of money.'

'How, sir?'

'*How?* I dunno! However you like! You saw it through the window—in a club or pub—in the full light of the broad highway, if you prefer: I've known magistrates believe that . . . and funnily enough, in my experience it's even happened. These ponces get over-confident after a while and take unbelievable chances.'

'No, sir.'

'Eh?'

'I want to ask you take me off this case, sir.'

'Oh, *do* you.'

'Yes, sir.'

The senior officer looked very hard indeed at Edward. 'Tell me,' he said quietly. 'When you saw this ponce alone in the cells, did he make you any promises?'

'Such as what, sir?'

'Now—be very careful. I've gone with you a long way, but please don't start getting cheeky. Has he made any promises of payment later on?'

'No, sir.'

'Are you quite positive of that?'

'Yes, sir. He's offered me no money, and I've not agreed to accept any from him.'

'Oh, I see. But you did discuss the matter.'

'We spoke of money in a general way: but no arrangements were made of any kind, sir.'

'Did *you* make *him* any promises?'

Edward—enticed by the fatal mistake of *liking* the Detective-sergeant and of wishing to be entirely frank with him—said, 'I did promise, sir, if this theft charge had gone through, to try to make it lighter for the girl than him.'

'Why?'

'He wanted it that way, sir.'

'*Did* he! So this man *wants* to get inside the nick—is that it?'

'Not on a poncing charge, sir, naturally.'

The Detective-sergeant paused, looked at Edward in an absorbed, impersonal way then said, 'Constable, this is it. You're chief witness for the prosecution again this man—or else.'

Edward replied in a low voice, 'I wish to submit to you, sir, my resignation from the Force.'

'I can't accept it,' the Detective-sergeant instantly snapped back. 'You can forward it through channels, naturally, if you wish, but until it's agreed to or refused by the proper authorities you're still bound by your oath and still under my direct orders.'

Edward, without asking for permission, sat down on a chair. 'Don't force me to do this, sir,' he said.

The Detective-sergeant looked at him, then sat down slowly also at his desk. 'You know,' he said, 'I just can't make you out. This man hasn't got at you, you say. I don't believe he's offered you his woman, or you'd want her if he had. And you like your work—I mean you *enjoy* it, don't you?'

'There's nothing I like better, sir.'

'And you know personal feelings count as nothing when there's a job to be done?'

'I know that too, sir.'

'You're not *against* ponces going to jail by any chance, are you?'

'No, sir. That's where they belong. But I can't do it, sir, because of my girl I'm going to marry.'

'Oh? I thought I was helping you straighten all that out?'

'Please listen, sir,' said Edward carefully. 'She's pregnant, as you know. She also loves me a great deal. She knows how much I want to stay on in the Force, but that if she has the child I may be refused permission to marry her.'

'Well?'

'I'm afraid she might try to do away with it—an abortion, sir.'

'But look, constable! I understood you'd both decided to go ahead and take a chance on the permission coming through in time to rectify the situation.'

'Yes, sir, I know. But I'm afraid she won't believe we *will* get permission, and she'll destroy the child to safeguard my career. And if she does *that* for me, sir—then I think I'll lose her.'

'Why?'

'She'll cease to love me, sir.'

'Oh. Oh, I see.' The Detective-sergeant leant back reflecting, then said, 'You know, constable, it's *you* who's behaving a bit like a ponce now, isn't it?'

'Sir?'

'Hiding behind a woman's apron-strings? Protecting your livelihood by swinging your sex life on me?'

Edward was silent.

'And another thing,' said the Detective-sergeant. 'Why has this business of a pregnancy and all this talk of resigning only come up when I gave you your orders about this particular poncing case?' Edward still said nothing and his senior pressed the point hard home. 'Why didn't you mention resigning earlier on if you'd decided? It must have been in your mind . . .'

Edward said quietly, 'I only came to the decision then, sir.'

'Yeah?' The Detective-sergeant frowned and pondered. 'You're trying to lead me off the track,' he said. 'There's something at the bottom of all this—something to do with that fucking ponce.'

Edward was still silent.

'Look, boy,' said the Detective-sergeant who was really getting quite a bit exasperated. 'This thing has gone quite far enough. Here, as I see it, is the situation. I've given you an order and you say you don't want to obey it. Well! Resign by all means if you really think you want to. But meanwhile either you obey my order or, I'm sorry, but I'm going to suspend you.'

Edward got up, stood at attention and said, 'Then please suspend me, sir.'

The Detective-sergeant's face hardened. He also rose. 'In one minute from now, constable,' he said, 'I'm going to do just that. But before I do I want to make one thing very clear indeed. If I suspend you for disobeying a direct order, there'll be an enquiry. And if there's an enquiry there'll be a lot of things I'll find I have to say that I've been overlooking for you hitherto. Very well. Now, if this enquiry should go against you—as I think it will—it won't be resigning you'll be doing. It'll be dismissal, and perhaps even maybe worse. And a man *dismissed* from the Force, constable—well, he's the lowest of the low. He's lower than that ponce that you're so fond of.'

Edward stood rigid but at ease, still saying nothing.

'You're suspended, constable,' the Detective-sergeant said. 'Report to the Station-sergeant now accordingly.'

MR LOVE

FRANKIE, released on bail from the charge of living off immoral earnings, and waiting while his lawyers hoisted his case from the rough justice of the magistrate's court to the dangerous impartiality of a judge and jury, had met his former girl for a chat about it all at the drinking-club now fashionable in 'the game': the other having suffered an eclipse as these clubs do, rising and falling with the fickle inclinations of their clientele and the slow-grinding machinery of the law. She was as desirable as ever though perhaps a shade more *elderly*—a bit wiser to a world about which she was already far too wise. He was relaxed, resigned, and *saddened* as only those born innocent can be when by folly or misjudgment they have behaved in some way that violates this quality of their natures.

'My chances?' said Frankie, summing up the situation. 'Slender, but they exist. After all'—he pressed her hand—'I won't have the principal witness in the box against me.'

'If only your lawyers would let me speak *for* you, Frankie. Say you were a handsome, silly boy-friend who knew nothing and I never gave you anything. You sure that's no use to you at all?'

'Dear—who'd believe it? And they say the sight of a—excuse me —common prostitute speaking up for me will damn me as a ponce at once with any jury.'

'Yeah, I know. But I'm scared of that copper's evidence, honey, when you come up at the Sessions. It's always so thorough and so dam *convincing*.'

She drained her b. and s.—a drink which, now banished from stately clubs and homes where it so flourished in Edwardian times, survives in our day as a favourite of this very Edwardian profession. 'Which cops will it be, I wonder? That bastard who got the box, and I suppose the Kilburn kiddy.'

'He's bound to speak against me, honey. After all why shouldn't he? It's his graft.'

Frankie rose and leaned over to work the cigarette-machine behind her back. She reached for her bag, said, 'I've got florins,' but he smiled, bent down and clicked the bag shut, then undid the packet standing close beside her stool in the tenderly sexy posture of bar lovers: girl's face level with boy's belt. She took her fag, held it unlit, looked up at him and said, 'You really think, dear, you couldn't try to skip?'

'We've been into that. They've got my passport and they'll be watching me this time. I've thought of trying: stow away and get duff papers—it's not that difficult, I know. But it seems this thing is coming to me and I might as well take it on the chin.'

'The nick's the nick, dear, don't forget. And with a previous conviction for *that*, they can whip you in for nothing and get a judgment on you till the day you die.'

'I've thought of that.'

'*And*—can you travel, after? I mean, go anywhere? Once you've got a record, honey, you've got a record.'

'Yeah.'

'Frankie! I believe you *want* to go inside!'

'No . . . you think I'm crazy? But I don't mind telling you, baby, I *do* think it's written in my book.'

'Fuck that! And when you come out, dear. There'll be some loot?'

'Oh, sufficient. Though the lawyers are getting most of what I've had . . .'

'There'll be me, too, honey. I'll be your banker, never fear . . .'

Frankie looked at her and smiled. 'Never again,' he said. 'Baby, I've thought it over and it seems I'm really not the type.

'No? Well, darl, they all say that. They all say "never again" the first time they get nicked, and they all head straight back to the chicks when their bit of trouble's over.' Frankie was silent. 'You know, dear,' she went on, 'there's only one thing does really trouble me a bit. I believe if I'd had that kid of ours you really might have grown to love me.'

'D'you think so?'

'Yes, I do. I think you're the type of man who never loves a girl but loves a mother.'

'I don't know about mothers, babe,' he said, giving her a lipstick-avoiding kiss, 'but I do know you've been great to me—a good chick in bed, yes, but in many ways just like my flesh and blood—my sister.'

'Oh, thank you! Do you mind? Your sister! Well—what next?'

Frankie went over to replenish glasses, and glancing round the room he felt for the first time in what seemed so long a while quite *different* once again from all these people there: a non-ponce, in fact: a man whose sex life was once more his own absolute and un-disputed property. Not that he judged them in the slightest, being no hypocrite, nor given by nature to imagine that to judge one's fellows has anything much to do with having a real sense of justice. But he did feel altered: and he had, for the first time in his life, an informed opinion on the easy-money boys.

Looking up, he saw one of them who entered and seeing him, withdrew. This was the star ponce whom Frankie, quickly abandon-ing the glasses on an indignant table, caught up with at the stairs. 'Hullo, man,' he said. 'Where you been hiding yourself? I've been looking for you.'

'Hi, Francis. And you, man! Where *you* been, feller—have you been away?'

'Not *yet*,' said Frankie. 'But it seems I'm going to just because someone who got scared felt they had to speak up out of turn.'

'Oh, yeah? That so? That really so?'

'That really so. Without that one man's coward's word I'd be in Africa or South America by now.'

'You would? Well now, Francis! Please don't *stare* at *me* like that, old-timer. Why! The way you stand there, making insinuations and just threatening a bit, anyone who didn't know might take you for a copper!'

The star ponce (in whose life this scene had occurred more than once before) knew exactly what he had to do: and that was get his blow in first. The wronged and righteous party in a quarrel often makes the capital mistake of forgetting—if it's going to come down to a set-to—that the villain, being such, is likely to be quicker off the mark because to counteract the power of towering indignation, he has only speed and swift decision. At least six seconds before Frankie got in his knock-out punch the star ponce had bent, pulled the blade from its plastic sheath inside his nylon sock, and stabbed Frankie neatly in the groin.

MR JUSTICE

PREFERRING for reasons best known to himself (no doubt financial) to travel like the emigrants of old by sea, Edward's father-in-law-to-be set sail (seen off by Edward not so much to shed a parting tear as to make sure he *went*) from the grubby and antique shores of Fenchurch street railway station. Though his departure now seemed so much less important the thing, once set in motion, could not be stopped because his girl's Dad had grown fond of the idea, and neither Edward nor she regretted it. The older man was in high spirits, haloed already with the aura of a tropical remittance-man; and only subdued, as Edward was much more so, by anxiety about his daughter's critical condition: the night before, attacked by sudden pains, she had been carried off to hospital. 'Send me a radiogram, boy,' the father said, 'as soon as ever they tell you what it is. And if it's serious, even if I have to get off the ship at the first port of call—well, rely on me, I'll face the journey back across old Biscay.'

'I hope that won't be necessary,' said Edward.

'Me, too. But note down my cabin number all the same.'

Edward reached by long habit for his little book, took it out, looked at it, and wrote the number there.

'Well,' said the expatriate, 'I won't keep you any longer: I know you've got to fly back to your headquarters. Well, lad, there it is. Cheerioh! All the very best! And thanks for all you've done for me and all you're going to do.'

Repressing with great difficulty an overpowering desire to say, 'Farewell, you old bastard, and whatever you do, don't come back,' Edward said (using the word for the first time). 'Good-bye, Dad, and good luck.'

The men shook hands, waved and separated, and Edward made off to the underground. At the foot of the escalator he dropped the black note-book, after looking at it once again, in the litter basket there provided. As he travelled west the docile public in the carriage, massed in long-suffering wedges of impatient and resigned humanity, now seemed to him as they had often done since his suspension not the *them* they used to be, but *us*: an us he still disapproved of in so many respects and still mistrusted: a great, confused, messy, indeterminate 'us' in need of regulation, guidance from above and order.

He had made in the past weeks several visits to the station on routine matters concerning his three rather contradictory appeals (to resign, to get married, and against unjustified suspension), but had no longer been admitted to the inner chambers of his erstwhile protector the Detective-sergeant. But to see him an imperative summons had now come; and so after a brief, fruitless telephone call to the hospital where his girl had just been taken, he walked up the breeze-block stairs and knocked, at exactly the appointed hour, upon the door.

Within he found the Detective-sergeant and, now restored to health, his own Iago, the star sleuth. The Detective-sergeant, most unusually for him, was in uniform which somehow made him look, though more official, less redoubtable. The star sleuth was in neat expressionless plain-clothes. 'Sit down,' said the Detective-sergeant.

He picked up a file, then putting on spectacles (giving him the appearance of a modern British general) he said to Edward, 'I don't want to see you just at present, constable, and I dare say you don't want to see me. Unfortunately, though, we've both got to. It's about this ponce. He's been involved in an affray in addition to being on bail on a much more serious matter. I don't know the rights and

wrongs of it yet, but as it was a quarrel between ponces I don't suppose it very much matters either way. At all events, as he's out on
bail and subject to the jurisdiction of the courts we've had him put
into a hospital where we can keep an eye on him, so as to be ready
for him when *he's* ready to face either of these charges.'

Edward and the star sleuth, neither looking at the other, preserved a silence of the kind that indicated all this had so far
registered.

'Now, as regards the poncing charge,' said the Detective-sergeant
looking at Edward, 'if that comes up first we're calling you as a
prosecution witness. You can refuse to appear, of course, that's
entirely up to you, but if you do I'd suggest you take counsel's
opinion as to what your own legal position might then be. Is that
understood?'

'Yes, sir. I'm ready to testify.'

'Oh. You are?'

'Yes, sir. I've decided it's my duty to the Force even though I
have to leave it.'

'I'm not much interested in your motives, constable, any longer.
What I'm interested in is facts. Now. If you and your colleague here
are going to testify you'll have to get together and make sure your
statements correspond. We'll be up at the Sessions, don't forget,
with defending counsel and the whole bag of legal tricks. So I want
some co-operation so that you both get the whole thing absolutely
crystal clear within your two minds. What I *don't* want,' the
Detective-sergeant added, putting down the dossier, 'is any conflict
of evidence that might lead to an acquittal. I do *not* want, in short,
if you can grasp this, the Force to be made a fool of. Any questions?'

'No, sir.'

'You?'

'No, sir.'

'Very well. That's it. You can carry on.'

The telephone rang and the Detective-sergeant, answering, looked
up angrily. 'Constable,' he said to Edward. 'Did you tell them downstairs they were to put your private calls through to *my* office *here*?'

Edward got up. 'It's from the hospital, sir. My girl. She's very ill.'

'Oh. Oh, all right then. Take it.'

Edward picked up the apparatus, listened, hesitated, then said, 'Thank you. All right, thank you,' and put it down.

There was a short silence.

'Bad news?' said the Detective-sergeant, a faint glint of a former light appearing through the thunder on his brow.

'My girl's had a child, stillborn, sir.'

'Oh. Sorry, lad. Very sorry.'

The star sleuth said to Edward, 'I hope it's a natural miscarriage, not the other thing.'

Edward stared at him and tensed, but as he rushed the star sleuth saw him coming, and picking up a truncheon the Detective-sergeant used as a paper-weight he cracked it on Edward's skull between his eyes.

MR LOVE AND JUSTICE

THAN a prison there is only one place more impressive to the human spirit and even more a symbol of our mortal condition: a hospital. In prison there is the allegory of sin, punishment and (in theory at any rate) redemption. In a hospital, the deeper allegory of birth, death and (occasionally) resurrection.

Thus when respectable citizens pass by prisons (which they rarely do because jails are tucked away in improbable places) they avert their hearts and eyes from the reality that a prison is a particular extension of a society and not in any essential way a thing apart from it. And if one ponders upon prisons and, better still, goes inside one (other, of course, than as a visitor), one is forced to the conclusion that the prisoners are us: one fragment of those outside who save for chance and technicality might very well be inside; and that insofar as sin is universal all are criminals, even if not deemed so by the conventions of temporary self-invented laws.

But when it comes to hospitals the healthy man may avert his eyes and heart with greater trepidation: for birth, death and healing are by much more general consent our inescapable lot. And these beneficent places are, in their way, even more awe-inspiring because from the sentences they can pass there may be no release and no appeal on earth. And that is why the only place which coppers and criminals *really* fear are the white wards where those temporal imperfect figures, the screws and wardresses of the jails, become as guardians of something greater, the white-robed nurses and physicians.

As for the inmates, in either case they have a strong if momentary sense of solidarity. If you're in jail 'the others' is the world outside; if you're in hospital you belong to the fraternity of the sick—an aching body set apart from the community of the healthy beyond the disinfected walls. And it was not surprising that Frankie, convalescing from his wound on crutches, and Edward whose skull was healing likewise beneath an impressive turban of lint and bandages, should often have been thrown even closer together than their fates as healthy men had already brought them.

Their favourite rendezvous was the long sun-parlour where in this progressive establishment the walking-wounded were permitted to foregather, free from the martial disciplines of their wards, for chats, draughts, reading, at evenings telly-viewing, and for the calls by flower-laden visitors at the appointed hours. The nurses, in the brisk and bossy manner of their calling, came frequently to disturb the comfort and tranquility of the patients with thermometers and pills, and summonses to X-ray rooms and distant theatres, and charts to fill in with dots and crosses indicating such things as whether or not their charges had been, as they put it, 'good boys'. The doctors in their more remote and stately fashion made periodical forays, often, as with the colonel on his inspection, in files that indicated seniority and which trooper, in this army of good-health, held commissioned or non-commissioned status. But mostly the patients, attired in government dressing-gowns much too short for them (or else too long), were left to their own devices of boredom, pain, amity and tiffs.

Edward and Frankie had long ago put each other entirely 'in the picture' as to their respective pasts: the bonds of solitude, and ennui, and suffering, and even more the discovery that both were now outcasts from the law soon overcame any slight initial reluctance on either side. There was also the enormous interest and satisfaction of meeting 'the enemy' as equals on this neutral ground: as if they were two warriors of opposing camps interned, as a consequence of the misfortune of arms by some Swiss-like power, now pleased and eager with clear consciences to betray military secrets to each other.

When their two girls came to visit them in the evenings, the broken ice formed again ever so slightly: for these were both creatures from the outside world, living reminders of a troubled past and a most uncertain future. Not that either man was anxious or embarrassed by his own girl's behaviour to her sister: each woman had been most correct, and as the days passed even cordial; and the men learned to their astonishment, mild alarm, and then hilarity that the two girls carried on, outside the hospital, a certain degree of cautious social intercourse: phone calls, requests to convey parcels on a day either couldn't come and even joint excursions to their respective Odeons. And when both of the girls retired as the end of their visit was heralded by the clanging, by some eager authoritative nurse, of a bell that did more harm to broken nerves in a minute than the hours spent in the sun-parlour had healed, the two men gathered up the mags and fruit and fags they'd left, and laughed: though handing by mutual, unspoken agreement any *flowers* either girl had brought them to a horticulturist cleaning-woman to carry home. For each of them felt what many patients must have done—that it's a bit tactless of most kindly souls to bring flowers only when they visit hospitals, or graves.

Time after time they speculated on the days that lay ahead: chewing with joint professional gusto over every aspect of their own case and each other's. 'So Frankie, you don't think,' Edward said, 'you'll go down on either charge?'

'Honest, Ted, no, I don't. In the affray I was the victim, there were bags of witnesses and the feller's not marked at all himself, it seems. As soon as he comes up for trial I just can't see how they can bring me into it except as an absent witness with the affidavit that I gave them.'

'Yes, boy. But the other thing?'

'Well—you say you're out of the cowboy forces now. Of course, cop, I still don't believe you—not till I see you busted anyway, then I might. But even so I just can't see they've got the evidence, if, as you say, you've finally decided not to testify: and—remember this—the *longer* the thing's delayed the harder it is to prove.'

'Correct. What happened a year—even a month—ago convinces juries far less than what happened yesterday.'

'And what about you, boy? I'd say you're in the clear as well: dismissed, okay, but wedding bells and an honest job of some kind for the first time in your life.'

'Well, there's the enquiry I've still got to face, of course. But from what I gather although they think that officer acted within his rights by bashing me when I attacked him, they're not very pleased at it all happening inside a station. So they'll try to keep it very quiet. Otherwise, if they don't . . .' Edward's eyes gleamed slightly '. . . I might bring a civil action for assault.'

'You've been having a chat with your lawyers, too. I can see. And what of the future, sonny? What are you going to do?'

'I dunno: it's too early to say, really. Besides, outside my career I don't really *know* anything at all.'

'No coppers do.'

'Why should they? A job's a job. One thing I *had* thought of, though, is setting up with my wife when we get married in a dress-making business: that's her own trade, you see.'

'You'll need capital for that . . .'

'Well, we've got a little bit of that put by.'

'We won't ask from where. So—dressmaking: what does that mean? Little fitting-room upstairs? Places where the mugs who pay for the chicks' gowns can come in and admire their undies as they try them on?'

'I don't know about that.'

'While you and your missus go out and leave them alone there for a while? Boy, that's it! A little high-grade brothel's what your establishment will be.'

'Don't be foolish, Frankie.'

'I'm not! You'll see! The idea will grow on you.'

Edward drank reflectively from some repellent but no doubt curative beverage. 'And you, Frank,' he said. 'You'll be going back to sea?'

'Me? Oh, I'm not sure. As a matter of fact I've been turning the thing over and I think I might consider opening up a little investigation agency.'

'What does that mean?'

'You know—divorce and such-like. It's quite a busy trade and with hardly any overheads. I know a lot of the angles now and contacts, and it seems to me it's a possibility.'

'You'll have to be careful, sonny, that's all I have to say.'

'And so will you, son! We'll both of us have to be.'

An uneasiness in easy chairs, a creaking of un-oiled wheel-carriages, and a rapid extinction of pipes and cigarettes all signalled the evening visit of the house doctor. He was accompanied (as not in his formal, perilous visits to the wards by day when he came flanked by assistants and by students, and himself followed sometimes behind some mighty specialist) only and informally by the ward sister—a fierce and dreadfully cheery martinet whose days of maximum glory, as her huge, sexless, medalled breast bore witness, had been spent on hospital ships in time of war. The doctor himself was young, fair-haired, sharp, and amiable—a man of the new and blessedly rising school who believe that patients are best consulted, to obtain results, about themselves and no longer treated, in the style of some of the older physicians, as culpable and rather tiresome imbeciles.

'Having a natter?' the doctor said sitting down beside Frankie and Edward and, to the scandalized but respectful glare of the ward sister, offering them each a cigarette and taking one himself.

'That's about it, doc,' Frankie answered.

'It passes the time, sir,' Edward added.

'Your girls both well?' the doctor asked, a glance of friendly complicity coming into his sandy eyes.

They each said they were.

'Well, we hope to be turning you both loose among them before so very long,' the doctor continued, 'but please don't ask me *when* because, of course, only your specialists can give me the final okay for your release—*and* what's more we'll need the permission of the sister here.'

The three men smiled. The sister looked severe.

'Anyway,' said the doctor, rising, 'when you *do* get out you'll both have to take it easy for a bit: specially with the women and—this'll please you—work. You've both (his tone became suddenly professionally grave) sailed very close to the edge in your two very different ways. When you get your discharge come and see me, if you like, and I'll tell you all the gory details of just how bad you were. But not now. We want you to get fit, not turn into a pair of hypochondriacs.'

Left to themselves Frankie and Edward watched the night come on, a bit restive (as beasts are when they know the summons will soon be coming to the manger) and talking only spasmodically.

'You know,' Edward said, 'these hospitals are really terrific. All this goes on—all these people here—they treat you whoever you are —no questions asked—not even any money. Just so long as you're sick you're welcome. People should know about it,' he continued. 'People should know what goes on inside these places.'

'You might say, Ted,' said Frankie, 'they should know what goes on inside the cells and jails and station headquarters, too. Over in other countries where I've been and even in Europe on the Continent, thousands of people—and the very best among them—have had experience of the law from the inside on account of the political upheavals. But here everyone is so dam innocent: so simon-pure. They unload all their moral problems on to the law's shoulders and leave you boys to get on with doing just what you like in the public's name. Well, if they do that one day they'll wake up and find they've given you not physical authority but all their own moral authority as well.'

'Citizens,' said Edward, 'broadly speaking, just don't want to be responsible. I've always said that: they just don't want to know. They lack the sense of responsibility themselves and only the Force is left with any sense of obligation to the community.'

'That's just what I say, man! If you hear a scream in the night these days you say, "Oh, the law will take care of it". A hundred years ago or even fifty, our grandfathers would have grabbed hold of the poker and gone out and taken a look themselves. They'd have *done* something: not just dialled 999.'

'I guess that's the age we live in,' Edward said.

'Yes, but I don't like it, Ted. Because you cops—well, you'll switch to any boss: any boss whatever. Whoever's got a grip then you'll obey him however good or bad his acts and his ideas may be.'

'Well, Frankie, tell me! What else do people believe in any more but just authority! Whatever it may represent?'

'That's it: nothing at all! Not religions, anyway. As religions have got weaker coppers have got stronger—you ever noticed that? The cop is the priest of the twentieth-century world, inspiring fear and if you're obedient, giving you absolution. But there is one very, very big difference from the old religions. The god of the coppers *is* the copper: you're the priests of a religion without a god.'

In the gloaming Edward's face was indistinct and so was Frankie's and they talked in the direction of each other's voices. Edward said, 'If that is true, boy—and I really just don't know—all I can say is we coppers are exposed to very great moral stress: we have to deal more with Satan every day than the rest of you possibly ever dream of.'

The lights burst on and a high female voice cried, 'Beddy-byes! Come along, boys, or I'll have to spank your little bottoms! Back to your wards you go: last one turns off the telly—and the lights!'

Neither man moved—as much by disinclination as in rebellious assertion of their manhood. 'These nurses!' Frankie cried. 'The first thing I'm going to do when I get out is date *that* one and break her bloody heart for her!'

'I doubt if she'd be interested,' Edward said, returning from the light-switch where he'd gone to restore the soothing, healing twilight. 'I know you kill them, Frankie, but that one, I think you'd find she's wed to her sputum mugs and bedpans.'

'*All* chicks are interested,' Frankie said, 'unless they're frigid.'

'You sure of that? I think there are some who centre it all on their vocation or on just one single man.'

'Sex, boy, *is* a woman's chief vocation: and plenty of it.'

'Frankie: it ever occurred to you that your experience, really, is very limited?'

'Mine? Well! Well, if you say so, officer.'

'I mean this: you don't know about other kinds of women because you've never met them; and you've never met them because you're only interested in them if they play it your way.'

'Well—that may be. But you, Ted: you consider your experience is so varied, then?'

'No—not varied but I think it's deep.'

'*Deep*? Yeah? Excuse the question, boy. That girl of yours: she's not your one and only by any chance is she?'

'Yes.'

'I thought maybe so. You mean the only one you ever *had*?'

'Yes.'

'At your age? And you say *you*'ve got experience? And frankly, Ted: can I say this? that girl of yours: I know she's a loyal kid and worships you and all the rest of it but . . . well, she wears glasses! And she doesn't dress very sharp, now, does she? I mean, with a chick like that in spite of all her qualities I think you're bound to have a very blinkered vision.'

'If you wear blinkers, Frankie, you see straight: straight ahead and see where you're going to all on one track. I don't think it's real sex always to begin again and again with someone else: I don't think you add to it or build anything or go really deep.'

'That "deep" again: you've been in deep with that lass?'

'The longer it lasts the further we both seem to be from ever coming to the end of each other. I think real sex, Frankie, is quite simple: it's one girl.'

'But you've not tried others.'

'I still think what I say.'

'Well: real *love*, perhaps, if you like to call it that . . . but not real *sex*, feller—how can it possibly be?'

'I say real love *is* real sex: they're one and the same thing exactly; and you find them only in one and the same person. Break out of that and you destroy them both.'

'Well, Ted . . . all I can say is you may be correct but you can't really know that till you've tried.'

'Nor can you, Frankie, if what I say is so until *you*'ve tried it.'

Again the lights glared into flame. 'Naughty, naughty!' cried the nurse. 'Now, really! Into your beds at once you go the pair of you or I'll call sister and she'll have you both up on a fizzer before your specialists in the morning!'

Frankie and Edward rose in silence, and outside the swing door patted each other and shook hands. 'Don't die in the night,' said Frankie. 'Is that a promise?'

'And you, pal. No interfering with the night nurse, is that understood?'

They went their several ways along the dim-lit corridors. Peace settled on the hospital except for grunts and occasional sharp little cries, quickly suppressed.

In his office the size of a small bathroom, the house doctor had a cocoa with the ward sister.

'Disgusting stuff, sister,' he said smacking his lips. 'It's a shame to make the poor fellers drink it.'

'It's for their good, doctor,' she said. 'And a bit more of *that* and less of the other thing might do some good to *your* health, too.'

'Oh, doctors are never ill—didn't you know? Or nurses! You've learned that, sister, by now surely.'

The nurse, pursing her already purposeful lips, handed him two folders.

'Yes, those two,' he said. 'Quite astonishing recoveries the pair of them: they do us great credit—don't you think?'

'Us, yes *and* their specialist doctors,' said the loyal nurse.

'Oh—indeed: and dame nature, too. *This* one with the groin wound . . . well, do you know sister? I'll spare your blushes but to put it politely if it hadn't been for some crafty work on him by the specialist, that man would never have been able to love at all.'

'Better for him, perhaps. And the brain case?'

'Well, *him*—he's lucky, frankly, now to *have* a brain. If the specialist hadn't been on hand the night they brought him to us, this feller's judgment would have been seriously impaired for life.'

The ward sister took a decorous sip. 'And you think,' she said, 'that either of them will make good use of these two essential faculties?'

'Frankly no,' said the doctor cheerfully. 'Well, I mean obviously not! They're frail human creatures just like you and me—yes even you sister, I dare say. But at any rate we've given them back the spare parts that they need, and that's all a nurse and doctor—yes, and even a specialist—can do. The rest of it begins where healing always ends and life begins: *we* don't have to decide the use they'll make of their lives, thank God!'